THE AUTUMN ROAD TO THE ISLES

'Only the road and the dawn, the sun, the wind, and the rain,
And the watch fire under stars, and sleep, and the road again.'

JOHN MASEFIELD

THE AUTUMN ROAD
TO THE ISLES

by
'B B'

Illustrations by
DENYS WATKINS-PITCHFORD
ARCA FRSA

COLT BOOKS
Cambridge

COLT BOOKS LTD
9 Clarendon Road
Cambridge CB2 2BH
tel 01223 347047 fax 01223 365866

First published by Nicholas Kaye 1959

This edition first published by
Colt Books 2001

ISBN 0 905899 37 7

British Library Cataloguing in Publication Data
A catalogue record for this book is available from the
British Library

Printed and bound in Great Britain by
Biddles Ltd, *www.biddles.co.uk*

FOR MIKE AND MARCIA

DENYS WATKINS-PITCHFORD, or 'BB' as he is known, was born in 1905. He grew up in Northamptonshire, where he spent many hours out in the open air as ill health prevented him from being sent to boarding school. He studied art in Paris and at The Royal College of Art in London, and for seventeen years was art master at Rugby School. He was already illustrating books before he began to write under his pseudonym, 'BB'.

The Sportsman's Bedside Book (1937) was the first to carry these now famous initials, followed by *Wild Lone, the Story of a Pytchley Fox* (1939) and *Manka, The Sky Gypsy, The Story of a Wild Goose* (1939). He was awarded the Carnegie Medal for *The Little Grey Men* (1941), the tale of the last gnomes in England, which established him in the forefront of literature for children. Many titles followed for both adults and children, and his reputation as a naturalist was further enhanced by contributions to *The Field, Country Life* and *Shooting Times*. He died in 1990.

Contents

Illustrations

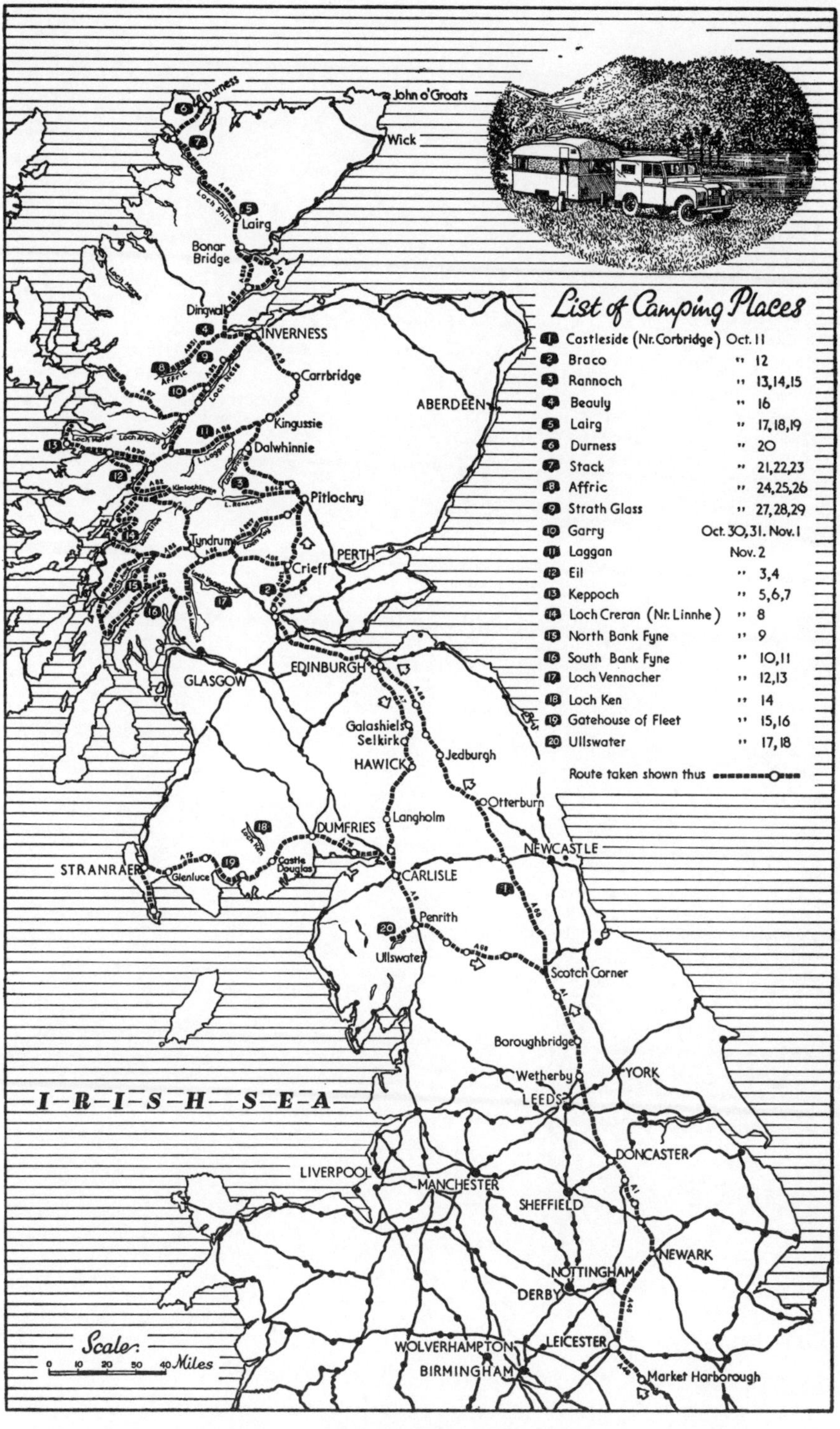

Map of the Journey

CHAPTER ONE

Twilight Encounter

THERE was a wicked little wind soughing over the sodden heather where the black peat cuttings shone wetly like the backs of slugs. The desolate moor, hummocky, and with outcrops of lichened granite, lay on my left, while beyond it rose the lower slopes of Ben Stack which climbed upwards into the rolling mists.

From those far slopes a sound came to me, one of the wildest sounds in nature—the belling of a stag. Those who have never heard the mating call of the wild red stag in the rutting season have no idea of its menacing quality. It is a bull-like noise, a low roar, followed by three or four grunting sounds which carry an immense distance on a still October night.

I left the road and walked across the heather. The water squelched and wheezed under my boots, and there arose a rich fragrance from the bog myrtle. A few tattered white shreds of cotton grass hung, like Tibetan prayer flags, from slender withered stems. No purple now upon these heather braes, but a deeper, richer dye, which to my eyes is more beautiful, for who can match the Rembrandtesque madders, umbers, siennas and old gold of the winter Highland moors?

The stag's challenge rang louder now, dead ahead of me, but in the fading light of the autumn dusk I could see little but the far lower screes, the loose boulders at the foot of the great mountain.

I leapt over the peat cuttings, passing, once, a peat cutter's heavy blade left bitten into the cheesy black rampart. I jumped narrow rushy rivulets, embryo burns which, hastening downwards among the bogs and myrtles, joined some main artery which drained into Loch Stack behind me.

There was a low hummock of heather ahead and the dull roaring of the stag seemed very near now, though at times it came and went as does the sound of church bells on a fitful breeze. I peeped over and slipped off the cover to my telescope. With the naked eye there was little to be seen, but once I snuggled down with the glass the picture was there in every detail. This is what I saw.

Some two hundred yards distant, perhaps a little more, was a narrow glen down which cascaded a white torrent; I could hear the sound of it swelling and fading like the rumble of a train.

Slender white-stemmed birches straggled up the sides, still in yellow leaf, and on the left of the glen, on a narrow grassy place, four hinds were quietly browsing, their coats wonderfully camouflaged against the broken deep tones of buff and brown of their surroundings. In front of them were six or seven woolly sheep, which, like the hinds, were browsing peacefully. Some twenty yards to the left of them, and nearer to me, was a great old stag; grey he was, with a rough mane and a fine head.

Just as I focussed my glasses on him he drew back his horns, raised his muzzle, and roared. I could see the steam jetting from his mouth.

What a picture that was! It was a scene which I shall carry with me until the end of my days, for it was one of the very things I

. . . raised his muzzle and roared'

had come to see, a challenging stag in his wild natural habitat.

For some minutes I lay watching him. He bellowed with neck outstretched, and horns well back, and then would stand again, feet together, ears spread, listening, looking, and the hinds fed on down the sloping green grass towards the burn.

I bellowed back, without showing myself, copying as well as I could the hoarse roar and the following grunts 'augh! augh!'

The effect was comical. All the hinds ceased feeding, each swung round, looking towards my hummock, their ears spread like sails, their dark eyes wide, nostrils working. The stag was rock-still, looking, too, towards the spot where I lay behind my little hill. Then he did a surprising thing. He swung round suddenly and galloped over to his hinds. With a sweep and lunge of his horns he turned them around and drove them up the steep little glen, chasing them for thirty yards or more. Then he turned back and went for the sheep, which all this time had been grazing peacefully on towards the burn.

They bobbed and bounced in mock terror, and as soon as he stopped they began to feed. This enraged him all the more. He went after them again. They leapt the burn, one behind the other, like animated mopheads, and resumed their feed on the other side.

The old fellow was now in a thoroughly bad temper, especially when I belled at him again. He came trotting back to his hummock and stood staring, like Landseer's picture, *The Monarch of the Glen*. His hinds were now suspicious. Each one was alerted with upturned face towards me and ears spread.

He belled once more, then with a final series of furious grunts, he came at a gallop towards me, kicking the spray sideways in white spurts as he came.

It was an alarming sight. There flitted through my mind something a stalker had told me a few days before of how the stags in the rutting season can sometimes be savage. During the stalking time they are as timid as rabbits but once it is finished and death lurks no longer behind rock and heather, they lose their induced fear of man.

I should have stood my ground to see what he would do but

some primeval fear made me turn and run. I glanced over my shoulder. He was still coming on; he had seen me now and was unafraid. Panting, I reached the road and looked back. Fifty yards away he was standing glaring at me and I saw the hair on his face and neck was as grey as lichen on a fallen pine.

I felt secure on the road. I know not why for it was a lonely one and the Landrover and caravan were half a mile distant, down among the whins beside the grey loch. He stood there watching me then, with another grunt which sounded very much like disgust, he turned round and walked slowly away towards his hinds.

* * *

The whole idea for an autumn journey to the remote Highlands of Scotland came from my wife. I had just been reading a fascinating book by an American author[1] describing how he and his wife made a journey across the continent of America following the tide of spring.

'What a pity we can't do something like that,' she said. 'Why don't we go up north as far as we can go and take the caravan?' I gently pointed out to her that, for one thing, Britain is so small that we should notice little change of climate and, besides, there was the size of our van to consider—the Queen Mary, we call her. When we are setting out there is as much preparation as when a liner leaves dock, and she needs a large area for berthing.

'And another thing,' I said, 'what about the cost, and who is to look after the chickens, and Granny, and the dogs?'

'Write to your publishers,' suggested Cecily, 'see what they say. Paint a glowing picture of what adventures we should have. Let's go next summer!'

I found myself saying, with some enthusiasm, 'No, not summer, that's not the time to see the Highlands. October's the time, October and November, when all the trippers have left the glens, the hotels are empty and the roads free!'

[1] Edwin Way Teale.

Immediately my mind began to get busy. Yes, by Heaven, what a revelation that could be! The gold in the glens, the sunsets, the grey loch water lapping, salmon leaping, and the great red stags. To journey on leisurely, stop where you please . . . the mountain ash trees with their deep red berries and splayed golden-fingered leaves tinged with pink . . . and oh! yes, indeed, the rare sweet scents of the hill winds, full of all the spices of the wild wet moors! The vision died. Our van just couldn't do it, it would take far too long to haul her right up there, it would mean dawdling along at twenty-five miles an hour. I saw different pictures then, the grimy industrial country, the Great North Road, the wet shining roofs of slate, the mining districts and their spoil heaps; and how in the world would we find any space to park Queen Mary? park her where we wanted to be on the loch shore, by the tumbling burn? No, it wouldn't do, and we couldn't afford to hire a smaller van; and anyway the publishers might not like the idea.

Next morning Cecily said, 'I had a dream last night. We're going on that trip, I saw the letter from your publisher.'

I knew then that we *would* be going. I had not forgotten the time when she dreamed that my brother's wife in Canada was ironing his back with a flat iron. The next day a letter had arrived saying that he had had a touch of lumbago and Ann had ironed his back. So that was why I knew the trip would come off.

* * *

There was still the question of the van. We must not consider taking Queen Mary, for even the AA shook their heads doubtfully when they knew the route we wanted to take. But I wrote to a well-known firm in Cardiff, telling them of the proposed trip, and they offered to loan us a new van for six weeks. We went down to Cardiff with the Landrover to collect it. For those who are interested in caravans this might well be the place to describe it, for it served us nobly without any faltering and we travelled some rough roads.

Its length was fifteen feet, its width six feet six inches, and it had an end kitchen, which, to those who are not caravanners, may convey little. In my opinion, an end kitchen is much more convenient for it leaves the rest of the space free for living and storage. There were four bunks which could be converted into a double and two single beds, and a hanging cupboard whose doors opened at night to form a partition, again a most useful feature in a family van. Another excellent arrangement in this model was the inside lavatory, an absolute boon in wet weather. Cooking was done by Calor gas which of course supplied the lighting too, two lamps, one at either end of the van. We found it beautifully built, trim as a ship, and the doors and cupboards fitted closely without jamming, a sure sign of good-class workmanship. Its greatest advantage (after our experience with the bigger vehicle) was the ease with which one could unhitch and turn round.

On the heavier models the van is wound off the towing ball by hydraulic gear, which is often tricky and takes some little time. With our Romeo we could lift it off the ball and turn the van with ease. This is essential when parking in a limited space where you have to come out the way you went in.

It might be thought that caravanning is hard work for the lady members of the party; that it is really no change from the usual round at home, of cooking, washing, and cleaning. Yet when one is 'on the road' these chores are not half the labour. One eats when one feels like it, and meals can be simple, though we ourselves are no believers in eating out of tins; fresh meat and vegetables are necessary in order to keep fit and well. Another popular fallacy is that caravanning is a cold business; in our Romeo, however, we carried a Valor paraffin heater, a drum of fuel in the Landrover, and also, incidentally, a four-gallon can of petrol in case of emergency.

There is a happy fraternal feeling between caravanners, and when one passes another on the road greetings are instinctively exchanged as by mariners at sea. Very many people who choose this form of holiday prefer recognized camping sites, but I must confess that I regard such places as horrific, and prefer to seek out secluded spots where one can be on one's own. To be able to choose one's pitch, away from fellow men, amidst the finest scenery imaginable, makes one feel a king. No house could be more cosy, yet if the site becomes boring one can be on one's way, as free as a wandering bird.

Not many years are left when one may do this; soon Acts will be passed prohibiting the parking of caravans unless in recognized camping sites, and then half the fun and adventure will be gone for ever. There are not many more rose buds to be gathered, and maybe in a year or two, a journey such as ours will be impossible.

The greatest advantage of all is perhaps the cheapness of this method of taking a holiday. I estimated that our trip cost us £43 including 10*s*. 6*d*. for site fees. A motoring holiday, staying at hotels (when you could find them), would have cost us over £200. It will be seen that it represents a considerable saving!

This, then, was to be our home for the duration of the trip. Domestic arrangements were made and settled. On 11 October 1958, a fine still autumn morning, the moment came when my hand wandered to the starter button of Winston the Landrover and the engine sprang to life. We were to travel more than three thousand miles before we passed once more along the drive to our house. The avenue of beeches, now aflame with autumn tints, would be naked to the winter winds.

CHAPTER TWO

By Loch Tummel and Loch Rannoch

I REMEMBER two pictures from the first two days of our journey. One, a magical effect of frosty fog lying over Carter Bar, and apparently disembodied hills floating high above a white blanket of fog, crowned with little fir trees, like a fragment of a Dürer engraving; the other, our first night's camp over the Border on a lay-by beyond the village of Braco in Perthshire.

It was almost dark when we finally came upon this site, for we had spent some wearisome miles working our way round the head of the Firth of Forth. It was a night of storm with black clouds racing, a river roaring below us in the valley, and the wind making another, louder, roar in the beeches across the road. As I stepped out of Winston I heard, unmistakably, the crying of wild geese and looking up I saw a wavering line of them hastening over, blown by the following wind. I heard them again next morning and saw them high in the sunlight heading for Loch Leven in the South.

The Lowlands of Scotland, with their fine sheltered lochs and rich farmlands, are tribal gathering grounds for wild geese in autumn. They come in September, but mostly in October, and they arrive from far Arctic lands where they were born. On the large estates they find sanctuary and are seldom molested, though some lairds have goose shoots once or twice during the winter season to placate the tenant farmers.

It had rained heavily during the night at Braco and its loud drumming on the roof had awakened us more than once. In those brief intervals when I lay awake listening to the storm, I heard the roar of the river below growing louder by the hour, and in the clear light of morning it was in full spate, the foam no longer white but crested and yellow.

A fine-looking rugged old man trudged by as we were having breakfast, with a rod over his shoulder and a bag slung behind him, and just before we pulled out of our lay-by, I saw him returning. His bag had a bulge, the strap cut deep into the shoulder of his mackintosh. He had been making the most of the spate, and the most of the tail end of the season too, for in a few days the trout-fishing season would be over until the spring.

Journeying on that morning through the rich pasture lands of Perthshire with their well-tended policies and neat plantations of fir, I was reminded of Dr Johnson's journey when he came this way in the autumn of 1773. He says 'from the banks of the Tweed to St Andrews I never saw a single tree and the variety of sun and shade is utterly unknown'.

We had not long been upon our way when a sinister jangling sound began from somewhere underneath the Landrover. This became worse as we neared Crieff and I deemed it wise to stop and investigate. The cause was a simple one. The day before we had bumped over Edinburgh's archaic cobblestones and the vibration had caused the metal heat-shield on the exhaust pipe to come adrift at one end. Each pothole and hollow in the road made the shield vibrate like a spring, hitting the pipe below. No matter,

On the road in the Sma' Glen

thought I, we are close to Crieff, and a garage will weld it in a moment. This could be done whilst Cecily went forth with the shopping bag for we had provisions to get and some tins of milk, . . . the only practical way of carrying milk on a camping trip.

To our surprise, when we arrived at last in that bright and sunny little town we found blinds drawn over shop windows, the butchers and fishmongers shuttered fast, and an almost funereal air about the place. A large garage in the main street was open, I was glad to see, and whilst the shield was being welded, I talked with the manager, a well-spruced, educated man, who became most interested in the trip we were making.

'Why are all your shops shut on a Monday?' I asked. 'Surely it isn't early closing day?'

'Och no! It's a public holiday, the October holiday,' he replied. And here I might say that the Scots have a charming and most sensible habit of awarding themselves 'public holidays' at all times, and on the most unexpected occasions. This was one of them and we could obtain no supplies whatever.

The sun shone as we went on our way towards Pitlochry, and soon entered the lovely Sma' Glen (which means the Narrow Glen) which gave us a real promise of beauty in store. Cloud shadows lay over the mountains to left and right, turning the distant peaks a rare plum blue, and the sun was winking brightly on the scrabbling burns which flashed in the sunlight, showing the full beauty of the dying bracken all about us.

The road climbed and wound its way to Loch na Craige for over 1,400 feet and from there descended to Amulree on the banks of the river Bran.

Seton Gordon, in his lovely *Highways and Byways in the Central Highlands* tells of an interesting old legend about a huge boulder which stands near the head of the Sma' Glen between the road and the river. It is known as Ossian's Stone, and the tradition is that Ossian, bard of the Gael, was buried there.

When General Wade's soldiers were making the road through Glen Almond nearby, in the eighteenth century, they dug under the stone and discovered some human bones. The people of the country 'to the number of three or four score men' arose and carried them away with many lamenting airs on their bagpipes. They took them to a wild recess in Glen Almond where they were reburied.

Apparently this large stone was directly in the way of the new road, and it was with great labour that it was moved with the aid of crow-bars, levers, and jacks. When the hollow was excavated the soldiers found a small cavity, roofed and walled with flat stones, which contained bones, ashes, and half-burned stalks of heath, which suggested that it might have been the funeral pyre of a high-ranking Roman officer. There was a Roman camp nearby at the south entrance to the glen.

The sun shone so warmly and the air was so soft, redolent of the heathery hills and the dying bracken, that we stopped awhile by the roadside in the Sma' Glen whilst I made several sketches of Winston and of Romeo, his unsullied paintwork gleaming, with the cloud shadows upon the mountains beyond. A little dipper was busy in a burn on the right of the road, bobbing on a mid-stream stone, his little white shirt-front showing vividly in the sunlight.

These quaint and lovable little birds, which remind one of an outsize wren, both by their manner of flight and the way they hold their diminutive tails, are true birds of the hill streams. It was most amusing to see him leap into the shallow water and hunt along among the stones with his back completely covered, to bob up some yards on and whirr to another stone. Not only do they resemble large black wrens, but their nests are similar in shape, domed, and with the entrance at the side. Their favourite site is under the arch of a bridge and they will use the same one year after year.

Whether or not there is any variation in the colouring of dippers I do not know, but I always fancy that the waistcoat of the Highland dipper is a much more vivid white than that of his English relation.

* * *

We came at last to Pitlochry, that favourite tourist centre. I wanted very much to visit the salmon ladder at the vast concrete power-station at the falls. Architecturally it is very fine, with bold modern sweeping lines. The ladder itself, up which the salmon travel, is a series of pens fed by a slanting pipe through which the river pours ceaselessly in a thundering torrent.

Alas! The heavy rain of the night before had coloured the river. When we descended the cellar-like steps to the narrow dank corridor of the ladder we could see no lordly salmon passing up, only swirling khaki water with now and then the whirling shadow of a twig or leaf behind the thick plate glass. When the water is clear this must be one of the most wonderful aquariums in Britain, unique in that the fish one sees making their way up are truly wild.

This fresh-water fishery laboratory was constructed about ten years ago and was, I believe, originally designed for research into the life history of the brown trout. Already one important fact has been discovered: that the brown trout, like the salmon, always return to the place of their birth when they are ready to spawn. Interesting facts about the life history of the salmon have also emerged, one of them being that only eleven per cent of salmon fry survive.

I looked in vain for someone on the spot to tell me more about this fascinating place, which every visitor to Pitlochry must be sure to see, but the great dam was apparently deserted. It was a 'public holiday' at Pitlochry too.

* * *

We took the road for Tummel and Rannoch, hooking left off the main Inverness road round a hairpin bend which I hardly thought we could take with Romeo in tow.

The afternoon was full of golden gleams. Red leaves wavered downwards as we passed along, resting gently in the hollow of Winston's spare wheel, and lay in drifts upon the road. A low mossy wall was on our left, below that the tumbling river, gleaming in the October haze, with spread shafts of sunlight making radiating bars between the tall slender stems of larch and pine. Our outfit seemed to fill the road but we met no traffic, only bairns returning from 'skule'.

'We're lucky,' I said to Cecily, 'if we *did* meet something here we'd have a job to pass.'

Hardly were the words out of my mouth when round the corner came a large blue charabanc! I swear this must have been the last excursion of the season. The trippers sat like fishes in a tin, some with paper bonnets, others with flat plate-like caps.

We came to sedate halt, bonnet to bonnet. The driver, a fat-faced, bad-tempered-looking man, in a white coat and peaked hat, sat at his wheel, moveless, unco-operative. I sat at Winston's wheel. We looked at each other. The plate caps jostled, the paper bonnets bobbed. The driver motioned with his hand, a sort of waving 'go-away' gesture, waving me back. How could I back with a caravan? I was at once reminded of a story a man told me. He was travelling a Highland road, narrow like this one, with a caravan in tow, and he met a large black Rolls. The Rolls would not back, nor would my friend.

'Very well,' he said, 'just as you wish. I have my house behind me, I can sleep comfortably tonight. Here I stay.' The Rolls it was that backed.

The plate caps and glengarries now began to emerge like insects from their nesting hole. They gathered in a cluster, filling the road.

'If you drive against the wall, mate, you'll clear us,' said the foremost Platecap, shutting one eye and squinting along our outfit. He had a friendly good-natured face and spoke with a Manchester twang. I got out and surveyed the position. The Landrover would clear, with inches to spare, but I wasn't sure about the van, which extended each side of us. Inch by inch I, edged in towards the wall. The driver was now beckoning me on.

'Come on,' shouted Platecap cheerfully, 'come on, you're OK, come on, lad.'

Cecily who had got out too, held up her hand. I put my foot down on the brake. There was a large mossy stone protruding from the wall near the top. She wrenched it out and sent it tumbling down the steep bank into the river below. Platecap pulled a face and shrugged. I let in the clutch and we crept on with, I swear, not a hand's thickness between Romeo's gleaming cream side and the brazen blue of that enormous charabanc. Even so we had been scarred. A lower stone we had not seen scored a neat line all along the van, as a burin cuts a line on a copper plate. It was our one and only scratch of the entire journey.

* * *

If there is a lovelier road than that which runs by Tummel and Rannoch, I would like to see it. The time to travel it is upon an afternoon in October when the sun is westering over the mighty Grampian range.

Where is there a view to equal the Queen's View? Silver shone Loch Tummel on that serene afternoon, lying unruffled between its woods and mountains, with every birch and beech afire with the double glow of dying leaf and dying sun. I could picture the Queen herself in her silks and satins, surrounded by her lords and ladies, standing where we stood.

On that September afternoon in 1884 she and Albert, with her ladies, and Lord Glenlyon following in another carriage, passed over the same bridge we had passed over. The road then being unfit for carriages, the royal party dismounted and walked on to the falls of Tummel. Can't you see the picture?

Beyond the bridge carriages wait, there is the chink of harness as satin-coated horses toss their proud heads, and the coachmen and postillions stand idly about, awaiting the return of the royal company, whilst robins sing from the hazels.

Albert remarks tritely that 'the chief beauty of the mountain scenery consists in its frequent changes'.

'We got home,' the Queen says, 'at half past six; the day was fast fading, the lights lovely.'

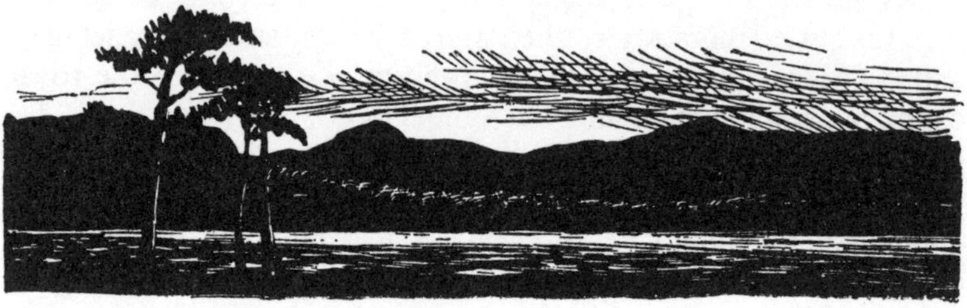

CHAPTER THREE

On the Shores of Rannoch

'THE day was fast fading and the lights were lovely' when we sought out our camping ground on the shores of Rannoch. This choosing of a suitable spot was ever a source of excitement and sometimes anxiety, especially when we had been travelling some distance and were near the day's end. One had to have three things; a good pull in and out, which meant room to manoeuvre, and a hard surface; a pleasant view, preferably by a loch or river; and fresh water within easy walking distance of the van, for it is no fun carrying heavy water-containers over rough ground. It was not always easy to find such a spot, and sometimes we motored many miles without finding what we wanted. On Rannoch, however, we were lucky. Beside the narrow road close to a little burn, which came gushing under a stone bridge, there was a wide grassy verge on to which we could roll without difficulty. We had around us a screen of small birch, a delightful grove, whose leaves had turned that delicate amber so characteristic of this tree.

Not twenty yards from us the waters of the loch swilled and played amongst the smooth boulders, and we could look across to the southern shore and its impressive mountains: Carn Mairg 3,419 feet, Schiehallion 3,547 feet (too symmetrical a peak for my liking), and much of the Grampian range. There was no snow as yet upon those highest peaks but they appeared dark and menacing against the sky.

Having connected the gas and made the lamps ready, we sat down to tea, and from the window I looked out across the grey waters which lapped so gently on the stones. I'd hardly begun cracking the top of an egg when a sudden shaft of evening light, as bright and concentrated as the headlamps of a car, shot across

the loch and shone upon our little bay. A graceful clump of birches grew there and the low ray of light set all their leaves aglow and their delicate silvery stems made a vivid contrast to the sombre tones behind. It was such a sudden and lovely picture I reached down my colour camera from the shelf above my head, and tumbled out on the shore. Almost as soon as I had clicked the trigger the light was shut out. I'd bagged it in the nick of time.

Those who have done any colour photography will know how important it is to have your camera loaded and ready to hand. Sometimes you must strike as you would a fish; delay a moment, and the effect has gone. There was an example of this later in our trip when we were passing over that desolate stretch above Loch Shin in Sutherland. We were nearing the head of Shin and the foreground bog grasses and little stunted mountain ash trees were full of vivid colour, whilst behind a brooding storm was coming up from the sea. Suddenly, a rainbow formed, arching over the wine-dark mountains in the distance. The left leg of it was straddling a little wooded corrie. Though I stopped the Landrover at once and jumped out, I was too late. By the time I'd set the exposure and raised the little camera to my eye, the rainbow had faded away and the foreground ceased to glow.

The wonderfully true colours of modern transparencies are almost unbelievably good and, indeed, are a great help to the artist. It is an expensive hobby, but though twelve shillings for an eight-film roll seems a lot, it does cover the cost of printing too. If one wishes permanent pictures to be made from transparencies it can be done, but they are invariably very disappointing and the prints cannot be compared with the originals whose vividness of detail and colour are almost 3D.

One of the first things we noticed about Rannoch was its absence of bird life. There may be more in spring and in the breeding season, but I saw no ducks. The only birds beside the loch itself appeared to be dippers and, of course, we soon had an attendant robin in the birches. I do not think there was a single camp that we had in a wooded district where a robin did not appear after a short interval. They are extremely jealous of their territories and what we take for friendliness is really quite the reverse. They inspect you with, I am sure, a jaundiced eye, like a gamekeeper views all trippers.

The level of Rannoch, as with so many other of the Highland lochs, has been raised by dams. The Hydroelectric people are very busy everywhere in this northern land, harnessing the waters for electric power. The result is that the trees which grew along the old loch shore are now partly submerged, to half way up their trunks. On Rannoch this was very marked, but the trees were still very much alive, possibly because they were alders which rejoice to have water at their roots. Gradually they die, however, for they

A buzzard by the burn

are continually buffeted by the quite considerable waves which beat upon them.

The suddenness of wind storms in the mountain regions is very noticeable. On Rannoch, during our stay, we had days of flat calm with scarce a ripple save that made by rising fish, but within a few minutes dark clouds would come over the Grampians, white horses would be rearing out on the open loch, and miniature combers would be breaking noisily on the stones.

One morning when the sun was shining brightly, and the loch lay glassy calm, ringed all over with rising trout, an inky black storm came racing up from over Rannoch Moor. White rollers were soon tumbling white foam on to the shore in front of us, and a magnificent rainbow sprang out, one stupendous bow against the inky sky. I was ready with my camera that time, and I got my picture.

* * *

This sudden bustling of waves on Rannoch's shore put me in mind of some of the lovely Gaelic names which are so full of poetry and the wildness of this land.

Listen to them. Loch-na-gar means 'outcry of the wind among the rocks'. Achnacarry, 'field of the fish weir', a' Chaorainn, 'hill of the rowan tree', Elrick, 'hill of the deer defile'.

They have something about them which remind one of the old Indian place names, many of which commemorate some successful hunt or dramatic episode of chase or battle, long-forgotten and buried in the past. Some stir the imagination in another way. One knows at once there was some strange legend about a certain hill, pass, burn or river. What, for instance, gave rise to Dun t-Soilcheig, 'fort of the snail'? Glen Affric, where we were later to have one of our most delectable camps, means 'glen of the dappled ford'; one can almost see the spotted stones, the glinting stars of sunlight catching the ripples, and the sound of it softly purling.

Some have a sinister ring such as Gobha Crom Bent or 'stooping blacksmith'; Gleann Bualtachan, 'glen of the striking'; and Bodach Lamh-dhearg, 'old man of the red hand'.

The shores of Rannoch

What was the story behind Leac nan Cuarain, which means 'flat rock of the sandals'? Sgor Ghaoith is descriptive for it means 'peak of the wind'. What of Caisteal a Chuilein Chruta, 'castle of the cursed whelp'? This almost smells of witchcraft, as does Leannan Sithean, 'fairy lover'; and Sithean a' Chatha, 'fairy hillock of the flight'. How one would like to know the story of Deor a Bhearnain, 'exile of the little gapped one'!

However, it is the better-known place names which really stir me; they ring on the ear like trumpet calls to battle and adventure. Staffa! Knoydart! Morven! Kylestrome! Badenoch! Listen to the music of the waves about the Skerries and smell the weed tangle in 'the Isles of Treshnish'. There is a hint of darkness and storm in Morar. There is something remote and splendid when we read Wester Ross; we see snow and stern majesty in Torridon, and the calm of evening in Firth of Lorne. But most of all I like the districts which take their names from ancient chieftains, Lochiel's Country, the Clanranald Country, and many more; and what pictures are conjured up by the Land of Moidart, and Brae Lochaber, which is that district east of Fort William!

There must surely be times when exiles from Scotland, on hearing these names, must feel strange, haunting pangs of home-sickness? In many a distant land, do not Scotsmen, of whatever clan, feel often a tug at their heart-strings, and an almost unbearable longing to return? Can you wonder that a country which bears such proud names compels undying allegiance from its sons and daughters?

* * *

We pulled out from our Rannoch pitch on the morning of 15 October intending to retrace our steps back to the Inverness road. Sudden black rainstorms had made everything wet and slippery and I had to watch for a lessening of the rain before I hitched Romeo on to the towing ball of the Landrover. Just as we pulled sluggishly off the grass, the sun came out and set every raindrop dancing on the bracken and trees. I had the Landrover in bottom gear but even so we could hardly pull the van on to the road. At a small rise a few yards on we stalled completely.

'Engine's cold,' said Cecily, 'better warm her up a bit.' I thought this a sensible suggestion, as we had not had the engine going for the last two days. So we sat patiently revving her up whilst Ping, the Peke pup, 'bubblebuzzed' the back of my neck, The engine now running without falter, I let in the clutch again. but it was as if we were pulling a dead weight behind us, and the engine 'conked' a second time. We got out and examined the coupling. Then we saw that the brake lever, which operates a steel wire, had not gone right down. The trigger had somehow dropped and caught in the ratchet which meant we were trying to pull against the brake. This being remedied, we went off once more, and for a few miles we seemed to be doing well. Yet something told me all was not quite as it should be; Winston was still sluggish, and I thought I detected a rather alarming smell, a sinister smell of hot metal. Dense clouds of greenish smoke were coming from the wheel hubs of Romeo and when I felt the brake drums they were almost red hot. The wretched lever had been jogged on again, and we had practically run Romeo's wheel-hubs dry of oil!

After fixing the lever securely so there was not the slightest chance of its going again, we crept up the pass of Killiecrankie to Blair Atholl where we stopped at the first garage in the town. Both wheel-hubs were quite dry and too hot to touch, and had to be repacked with grease.

This was a narrow escape for had we gone on, the wheels of the caravan would have seized, and we should have had great difficulty in getting spares.

CHAPTER FOUR

North to Beauly

THE road from Kingussie to Aviemore made us think of winter. Perhaps it was because the sun had gone and dark rainstorms swept across the high mountains to the west. Here, too, the moorlands were dark madder and ashy brown, the birches blown bare of leaves. Only the oak woods were thick in leaf. As we neared Moy we passed a lochan hard by the road. I call it a lochan (but it is called Loch Moy) and upon it, cruising 'midst slender ash-buff reeds, were several whooper swans. The true wild swan is not to be confused with the mute, which has a black knob on its bill, an arched neck, and is becoming a general pest in the south. They have no enemies and few sportsmen will shoot a swan, wild or tame, and they multiply each year and are an awful nuisance in fishing waters. Curiously enough, I had seen whoopers on this loch many years ago when I travelled this road. Many people seem unable to tell the difference between a wild swan and a tame one, yet there can be no mistaking the two. The wild whooper holds his neck perfectly straight, like a walking stick, and his head is long and narrow, the bill a rather wonderful clear, canary yellow with a black wedge.

We were to see many hundreds of whoopers later on during our journey; on some of the sea inlets on the eastern seaboard the herds run into many hundreds. I believe they, like our mute swan, are on the increase.

There has always been a superstition among the Scots about shooting wild swans, though St John, that doughty sportsman, who was a sort of latter-day Colonel Hawker, and of whom I shall have more to say later, describes many forays after them in the country around Nairn and in Sutherland. Not all Scots wildfowlers are so superstitious. I remember a story told me by a wildfowling friend who was out on one of the Northern firths after geese.

He came upon an old man sitting in a bog and he was sitting on the still warm body of a swan. My friend was, rightly, rather shocked. 'Surely you can't eat wild swans?' he said. 'Och no! I dinna eat them, but I hadna' anything to *sit on*, so I shot it.'

Wild swans, both whoopers and Berwicks (which are smaller) are coming farther south now that so many large reservoirs are being constructed. On the new reservoir at Pitsford, near Northampton, I have lately seen both species during the winter months. A few pairs of whoopers nest in Scotland each year, and they have even attempted to do so in Norfolk, but they are true winter visitors and breed in northern Europe.

I well remember in the winter of 1957, when I was out after duck one January dusk, hearing a number of whoopers coming over my head in a thick fog. This fog had come down quite suddenly and visibility was not more than a few yards. Somewhere on the flat fields to the north of where I stood on the bank of a river, a large gaggle of greylags were making a tremendous uproar (all wildfowl dislike fog), and just as I was thinking, and hoping, some would come my way, I heard the wonderful bugling musical notes of a herd of whoopers. They were evidently trying to follow the course of the river for they passed right overhead and I could hear the thresh of their wide wings. The strange unearthly musical notes awakened memories deep within me which must have been handed down from generation to generation, back to the time when our ancestors hunted these great wildfowl with the bow. I have no doubt that wild swans are excellent eating when they have been feeding inland, but I would not care to eat one on the coast, when they have been feeding on the sea grasses.

There have been a number of occasions when I could have shot whoopers on my fowling expeditions to the Ross and Cromarty area but I have never done so. There is just something about them which sets them apart from other fowl, such as the grey geese and ducks.

Travelling again upon the road to Aviemore I was reminded of the last time I came this way some twenty years ago. It was mid-winter then, and deep snow covered the high tops. On the summit of Carn na Easgainn a stag was pawing at the snow, sending the white powder back between his legs, and beyond him were a few dejected hinds. On that day too I saw my first golden eagle which flapped majestically across the road near Findhorn bridge.

* * *

Somewhere between Inverness and Beauly we took a road which led into higher wooded ground and at last came to a small hamlet beside a fine tree-filled valley where huge beeches grew and a burn roared hoarsely in the glen below. Beside what appeared to be a village smithy was a gate opening into a small green meadow under the shadow of tall beechen woods, floored with red and dying bracken. The owner, Mr Fraser, welcomed us there for the night, and though it went against the grain—stooping so low as to spend a single penny on a camp site—we were so weary that we turned into the field with thankfulness and parked the van on the far side, within earshot of the burn and close to the huge beeches. Later, in the wood, I found growing the most deadly collection of fungi imaginable: scores of Death Cap, and the

A roebuck in the glen

brilliant Fly Agaric growing side by side among the fallen red beech leaves, together with four or five other species, purple and gold in colour and shaped like elfin trumpets.

The night fell quickly, with sheets of cold rain and sudden gusts of wind. In our van we experienced a sense of cosiness and contentment for the stove was going, the lamps lit, and Cecily soon had supper cooking, though I think we felt a pang for our lovely Rannoch site. Ping too was glad to reach her journey's end, and for the first time that day could relax. She knew, when we were on the shores of Rannoch that morning, that we were on the

move, for she sat shivering miserably on one of the bunks, looking at us with goggly mournful eyes.

Dogs know at once if their loved ones are planning departure; how this is so I cannot say. Possibly something in the urgent bustling gives them some clue. We had done about 115 miles that day and the stern and wild was yet to come. I think we had all found this stormy journey rather wearisome, but once into camp, with supper on the table, we felt refreshed and infused with vigour. The supper Cecily laid on was the best yet: kidneys and bacon, potatoes and fresh cabbage, followed by tangerine segments, and this repast was accompanied by an excellent bottle of red burgundy which I broached for the occasion.

It was a strange night in our sequestered meadow. At times it was still, with no movement in the beech leaves hard by the camp;

then suddenly a terrific gust of wind, like the blast from an explosion, would rock the van and tear among the trees.

* * *

I suppose the city dweller rarely notices the sound of the wind, but there is a certain pleasure in being in cosy shelter, rested and warm, lingering between wakefulness and sleep; that time when one's thoughts begin to wander like erring sheep, and a vast contentment fills one's being.

I have heard the voice of the wind in many wild places on my wanderings, and its music varies with the time of the year. When the leaves are stripped from the trees it sings a keener, fiercer, tune; in a great wood that is in full leaf, it has a dramatic quality.

W. H. Hudson wrote some delightful passages about the sound of the wind in Savernake forest in Wiltshire, and as I lay that night listening to the great beeches just behind us, singing and thrumming like giant harps, I began to think of other writers who have spoken even more eloquently than did Hudson about the sound of the wind in trees. Edwin Muir, that fine naturalist, once wrote a memorable description of wind in a forest. To enjoy it better with all his being, he climbed a Douglas spruce:

> 'After cautiously casting about, I made choice of the tallest of a group of spruces that were growing close together, like a tuft of grass, no one of which seemed likely to fall unless all the rest fell with it. Though comparatively young, they were about a hundred feet high, and their lithe brushy tops were rocking and swirling in wild ecstasy. Being accustomed to climbing trees when making botanical studies, I experienced no difficulty in reaching the top of this one, and never before did I enjoy so noble an exhilaration of motion. The slender tops fairly flapped and swished in the passionate torrent, bending and swirling backward and forward, round and round, tracing indescribable combinations of vertical and horizontal curves while I clung with muscles firm braced, like a bobolink on a reed.

'In its widest sweeps my tree-top described an arc of twenty to thirty degrees. Now my eye roved over the piny hills and dales as over fields of waving corn, and felt the light running in ripples and broad swelling undulations across valleys from ridge to ridge, as the shining foliage was stirred by corresponding waves of air. Oftentimes these waves of reflected light would break suddenly into a kind of beaten foam, and again, after chasing one another in regular order, they would seem to bend forward in concentric curves and disappear on some hillside, like sea waves on a shelving shore. The quality of light reflected from the bent needles was so great as to make whole groves appear as if covered with snow, while the black shadows beneath the trees greatly enhanced the effect of the silvery splendour. . . . The sounds of the storm corresponded gloriously with this wild exuberance of light and motion. The profound bass of the naked branches and boles blooming like waterfalls, the quick, tense, vibrations of the pine needles, now rising to a shrill whistling hiss, now falling to a silky murmur . . . all this was heard in easy analysis when the attention was calmly bent.

'I kept my lofty perch for hours, frequently closing my eyes to enjoy the music by itself, or to feast quietly on the delicious fragrance that was streaming past.'

After recalling Muir's description, I fell to thinking of the sound of the wind in the acres of tall reeds of a Northern estuary where often I have waited for the wild geese to take flight at the first crack of dawn. This is a different music, more sibilant, perhaps more like the rustling of silken garments.

Uncountable millions of polished stems, darkly jointed, and immensely strong, crowned on their slender heads by dark feathered plumes, bend and bend again at each caress of wind. Sometimes when the gusts are fierce they bow right over, all twelve feet of them, so that their dark soft plumes brush the lower sedges. I have at times walked amongst them in the darkness before dawn and seen roosting starlings, like strange black fruit, clasped to the slender swaying stems. Putting out my hand I have gently plucked off the sleeping birds and held them, squawking outrageously, until I have let them fly. These great reed beds are beautifully warm and make a cosy dormitory for other species, like tits, wrens, and finches.

CHAPTER FIVE

To Lairg and Shin

THE Reay country in late autumn and winter is a golden land. Mile upon mile of treeless moor where the bog grasses deceive the eye with their brilliance, so much so that you think the sun is shining, even when the skies are grey and heavy with rain. The wetter the moor, the richer the colour, the deeper the glow of gold.

We came to Lairg in the forenoon by way of the high road by Achinduich for we had been advised the surface was better and the road less narrow. What a strange little place it is, with such a naked feel about it! The houses seem to crouch low with upturned coat collars, and now the level of Loch Shin has been raised by the new dam at the eastern end, the waters appear to be on a level with the village street, an arrangement which appeared popular with many white ducks and geese.

All about are the vast naked hills almost treeless but gold, gold as a bracken floor.

* * *

'D'you see yon hills over there?' said the man who filled my petrol tank, pointing across the grey waters beyond the dam. 'In hard weather I've seen them moving with deer, desperate, starving, and they die by hundreds. I think it a pity the owners of the forests don't put down food for them, the puir beasts.'

But it is hardly practical to feed the vast and starving armies, nor would it be wise. Nobody knows exactly the total head of deer in the Highlands. I have heard it put at 100,000 and this was probably near the mark ten years ago. But the Headstalker at Glenshiel tells me that this number can now be halved. The severe winters of '47 and '51 played havoc and thousands perished on the hills. Also, he says that the poaching gangs now operating in Ross and Caithness account for 'unbelievable numbers', to use his own words.

That eminent authority on red deer, Frank Wallace, has some interesting things to say about this subject in his book *Happier Years*. He was Deer Control Officer during the war, and though he writes of conditions over ten years ago, the figures he quotes of the number of deer killed by sportsmen give some idea of the numbers which can fall to the rifle in a season. In 1939–40, 7,130 stags were killed and 10,971 hinds. In 1940–41, 9,890 stags, and 12,844 hinds were shot. Many more would be killed by poachers and unauthorized persons.

A severe winter plays havoc with the stock. It was estimated that in the severe weather of '40–41 no less than 20,000 perished from starvation. It must be remembered by the layman that the wild red deer have no enemies other than man, and if their numbers are not kept within bounds by shooting, these enormous losses in bad winters are necessary if a healthy stock is to survive. Mr Wallace considered then that more stags and hinds should be shot, and that land overrun by them should be put to more profitable use; I have no doubt this applies today.

There is still a lot of poaching by motor gangs, despite the increased penalties. This is especially so in Sutherland. These gentry operate at night, many use submachine guns, and the beasts are shot in the light of the headlamps of their vehicles. Many are wounded and go away to die miserable and agonizing deaths. The 'rifle' will always follow up a wounded deer and see it is put out of its misery, but animals wounded by the poaching gangs are written off and abandoned. Most of the poached venison goes south. One can buy it in Perth and Dundee but I was unable to get any in the far north.

I had seen a pretty sight a little earlier on that wild and barren road which leads to Loch Naver and Reay. Three or four slow-moving cows were grazing by the roadside near a farm and with them was a delightful red deer hind, who showed no fear when I stopped the Landrover and held out my hand to her. She stood looking at us with dark wide eyes and with ears fanned, but she was less afraid than the cows, and much more curious as to who I was, and why I had bothered to stop.

Two years before she had been found as a tiny calf far out on the golden plain and brought home by the shepherd and reared with the calves. Now the cows are her sole companions, nor does she ever show signs of wanting to wander away. There was nothing to stop her, no fence, no tether, the byre was her home along with her slow-moving friends.

* * *

'What difference has the dam made to the fishing?' I asked a man who was mending a fence just outside Lairg.

'Better, better than ever,' he said, 'and the brown trout seem to be bigger now than ever before. June is the best month, and brown trout of four and five pounds are common, though one has better sport from a boat.' The fishing, I was told, was free to the visitor, and it seemed to me that Lairg might be worth exploring by any keen angler who likes his baskets heavy.

* * *

The head of Shin

We made our camp some two miles north of the village, parking our van on a strip of old road beside the loch where some little beech trees served as our only screen from the wind which was blowing, fiercely and piercingly cold from the north. Near Beauly we had seen the high mountains to the west sheeted in snow, the first we had seen that winter. Though without the sequestered beauty of Rannoch, this new pitch was certainly a good one, probably the best that could be found within a radius of a mile or two of the village. We were well away from the main road and felt secure. Only another forty miles lay between us and the northernmost coast of Scotland.

I had bought a small blue and silver trout spinner in Beauly. Though the brown trout season was virtually over, I would have liked to catch a fish out of a Highland loch sometime during the expedition and the man had assured me that it was open to doubt whether brown trout were really forbidden game in the remote Highlands. I cannot imagine that the tinkers observe the game laws of the country (incidentally, I was told by the landlord of a pub in Bonar Bridge that in Caithness these vagrants are a menace as they roam about in gangs). There were signs of them close by our own camp at Lairg, bottles, tins, and one fine deep stew-pan which seemed quite sound and new-looking, and which I salvaged for a dog dish.

In the half-darkness one evening, Cecily, who was sitting in the window overlooking the road and loch, saw a dark figure gathering wood among the stunted birch and bracken not far from our camp. For some time we watched this mysterious stranger who was very active, climbing over the fence and entering the woods on the left of the road and returning, busy as a beaver, with his arms full of faggots. Soon darkness cloaked all and we could see nothing but the tossing beech leaves.

* * *

For the last few nights, Ping, having been put on the spare bunk and covered with her little blanket (she slept like an infant on her side with her head pillowed on her cushion), took to getting into our bed at 3 a.m., a performance which invariably woke us up. It was a form of blackmail for we decided that henceforth she had better sleep with us for the duration of the trip. She is an extremely jealous little person and if I so much as kissed my wife good morning as she lay beside me in bed, Ping was between us in a moment, placing her two front paws and then her round soft head

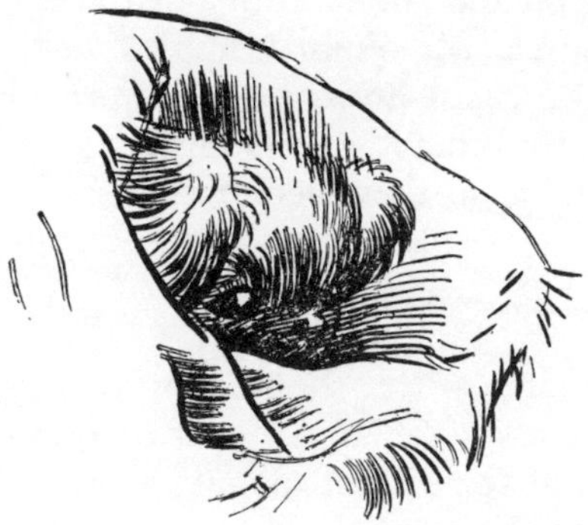

between our faces. Any affectionate demonstration brought immediate reactions. Even when she was at the far end of the van she would jump down and place herself between us as if to say, 'no more of this, *I'm* the only one to have any affection!' One great mystery was never solved by her—where we went when we withdrew to the lavatory compartment. She would sit with her round grapefruit head tilting first one side, and then the other, an anxious expression on her face.

The effects of sun-dappled golden machair and mountain along the Lairg-Durness road induced me to shoot off all eight films in my colour camera. Voyaging along, I would suddenly see a perfect picture, a scarlet-berried rowan leaning over a foaming burn, with lichened granite rocks, massive and grey; a flash of silver light on the broad waters of the loch, backed by towering grimly-dark mountains—every moment there were pictures.

We passed, one day, a tree-embowered shooting lodge where newly-flayed deer skins were hung on a fence to dry (I had noticed this too near Rannoch). I was intrigued by these skins, and later the Headstalker at Glenshiel told me that they are worth the surprisingly small sum of 5*s*. for a stag, and 3*s*. for a hind—only sixpence more than I used to get for moleskins when I was a boy!

They are hung on the fences to dry before being sent away to be made into gloves. Mr Colin Campbell tells me that thirty years ago, when buckskin breeches were worn, the skins fetched 15*s*. each which, by present day ratings, would be about thirty shillings a skin. Even so they were cheap.

* * *

By one of these lodges where the skins were arrayed like carpets put out to dry, we saw a tall Highlander in a deerstalker. He was levelling his glass at the distant mountain ridge. It was not long before we saw what he was spying. On the crest of the mountain on our left were thirty hinds and one magnificent stag. Through my glasses I saw him with head raised. Now and then he drew back his horns and bellowed a challenge, though we were too far off to hear his voice. There were little calves among his hinds and nearly all his ladies had their wide ears cocked, looking down at us in the valley.

We had a sumptuous dinner on our last night at Shin, a thick tender steak with fried onions. The steak we had bought in Lairg, the onions came from the garden at home. 'Home' did I say? It seemed another world, far removed in time and space! This now was our home, the trim little van, so light one could lift it from the towing ball on the Landrover with one hand and twiddle it round in next to no time.

The next morning the loch appeared as if it were frozen from bank to bank. Pillars of mist smoked upwards from the surface, moving slowly along the water. From the direction of Lairg came the wild tang of peat smoke on the wind, which, such as it was, was blowing towards us from the east. To my great delight, as I stood on our little grassy shore by the old drowned road, I saw a single greylag come winging down the loch. It passed near enough for me to see its heavy yellow bill. It was fairly low, only gunshot high, and it flew without sound. I watched it labouring away over the red-brown slopes of the hills on the west side, until it dwindled to nothing in the mists. Perhaps that wild goose was not a migrant but a true native, for not more than fifty miles to the west lay the Summer Isles where they still breed in a natural state. St John, in his *Wild Sports of the Highlands*, has this to say of Shin.

> 'In some parts of Sutherland, for instance on Loch Shin, and other lonely and unfrequented pieces of water, the wild goose breeds on the small islands that dot these waters. In a lonely and little-frequented spot on the banks of Loch Shin, where the remains of walls and short green herbage point out the site of some former sheiling long since gone to ruin, I have frequently found the wild goose with her brood.'

He describes these geese as Bean geese, which is now an uncommon species in Britain, but which were plentiful around the Findhorn district in early spring during the last century. It must be some years since any species of wild goose bred on Shin for the district cannot now be described as 'unfrequented'.

As I lay in bed earlier that morning and looked out at the canopy of green beech leaves, I had seen a cock chaffinch, a young bird of the year, sitting on a branch; obviously it had slept there among the thick leaves close by our bedroom window, and it seemed sleepy and only just awake. Maybe it had been hatched six months previously in the woods close by, or it may have been a migrant. Its plumage was puffed out for it was a very cold morning (even the interior of the van was cold despite the fact we had had a stove burning all night), and one leg was tucked in. It sat among the leaves looking about it, continually turning its head sideways to watch a procession of gulls which came down the loch every morning after sunrise. I thought I detected interest and wonder in its bright little window of an eye. Somehow I felt with it a bond of sympathy and compassion. Both of us were alive, each aware of the world, of the chilly autumn morning, of the tang of the peat smoke on the wind, of the coming of winter. For so short a space we may delight in the world around us, bird and man alike, each in his own way, and as long as we have health and strength all is in tune. There can be no higher pleasure than this, of leading and living a natural life, in bodily health, free from care, and, in a sense, free from responsibilities, at least for a while. To be with one's own loved one, complete and free, to be without newspapers, television, wireless, or telephone—that in itself was a refreshing thing. Rockets might circle the moon, men might war with one another, H bombs and other horrors might be detonated above and below the earth's crust: these things were beyond our knowledge, and beyond our caring!

The weather now assumed importance. It made some difference if it rained, or blew, or if the sun shone; if the nights were cold, or warm. We were closer to nature and the natural world. It is true that bad weather could not wet or chill us, in our snug, splendidly-constructed van, as it must affect wild creatures of mountain and moor; but the climatic conditions coloured our days and when the sun shone, turning the hills to a more vivid gold, it gave the greater pleasure.

* * *

To savour the Reay country in its every mood, one must get away into the hinterland of bog and moor and see the autumn dusk steal down. The brightness of the machair fades and takes on an awesome gloom, whilst far out in the sombre wastes, a lone lochan gleams back at the last of the day.

Everywhere the hoodie crows were plentiful, handsome birds with their grey mantles worn like monkish habits. They must surely be one of the commonest species in winter in the far north

Falls of Shin

and they must do considerable damage to the young grouse. On rare occasions I see them on passage in the midlands, and every winter they hunt the shorelines of the Wash.

I never see a hoodie but I think of some birds I saw scavenging on the quays of Riga. They were the same size as a hoodie and had the same markings on the back, but the mantle was pale biscuit-colour, not grey. I have never seen this bird figured in any bird book, not even in Roger Peterson's excellent handbook on the *Birds of Europe*. It is a little puzzling why this species should take the place of the carrion crow in the north. Their habits and general build are very similar, they are great scavengers too, and their voices identical. Any dead or mortally-wounded bird which falls to the fowler's shot is quickly attended to, for these crows are always hunting the tidelines of the Northern firths.

CHAPTER SIX

The Reay Country

GOLDEN gorse was starring the roadside banks as we journeyed on towards the sea. It was the Sabbath day, the sky was a soft dove grey, and droves of clucking fieldfares, so distinctive with their pale rumps, flew parallel with us as we climbed away above the bare shining expanse of Loch Shin.

I was reminded that Charles St John (we were now in his country) made an expedition through this part of Sutherland in 1848. Almost in the first few sentences of his book *A Tour in Sutherland* he says, with strange inconsistency, 'my object in making this journey was to enjoy the magnificent scenery of the north coast, and to see and observe the breeding habits of many of the rarer birds of Britain . . . not being a collector of eggs or birds myself, I had no wish to destroy more of my feathered friends than sufficed to prove their identity, and procure a few specimens for a gentleman who is as great a lover of nature as myself, and a far more scientific one'.

During that spring journey in 1848 he worked hard to exterminate his 'feathered friends', the osprey in particular, which even at that time was a rare bird in the Highlands. He was very successful. Near Scourie he heard of a loch on which a pair were nesting. Let us hear St John's own account:

> 'At the place the landlord mentioned—a small bridge about three miles from Scourie—we went to a point of rock from which we could command a view of the loch in question (This was no doubt Loch an Liag Aird to the south west of Laxford close to the sea.) We immediately, through the glass, discovered the nest of the osprey, built in exactly a similar situation to the last, that is, on the summit of a rock eight feet high, shaped like a truncated cone, and standing alone and exposed in the loch. On coming nearer we could distinguish the white head of the female osprey on the nest. The male bird was not in view. It was determined that I should remain concealed near the loch, whilst my two companions went for the boat. This plan was adopted for the double reason that I might be at hand to shoot any hooded crow who might attempt to take the eggs while the osprey was off, she having left the nest on our approach, and also that I might have the chance of shooting the old osprey herself in case she came within shot. I must say that I would rather she had escaped this fate, but as her skin was wanted, I agreed to kill her.
>
> 'For some time after the departure of my companions she flew round and round at a great height, occasionally drifting away with the high wind, and then returning to the loch. She passed two or three times, not very far from me, before I shot her. But at last I fired, and the poor bird, after wheeling blindly about for a few moments, fell far to leeward of me, and down amongst the most precipitous and rocky part of the mountain, quite dead. She was scarcely down behind the cliffs when I heard the cry of an osprey in a quite different direction, and on looking that way I saw the male bird flying up from a great distance. As he came nearer I could dis-

tinguish plainly with my glass that he was carrying a fish in his claws. On approaching he redoubled his cries, probably expecting the well-known answer, or signal of gratitude from his mate, but not hearing her, he flew on until he came directly over the nest. I could plainly see him turning his head from left to right, as if looking for her, and as if in astonishment at her unwonted silence. He came lower and lower, still holding the fish in his feet, which were stretched out at full length from his body. Not seeing her he again ascended and flew to the other end of the lake, the rocks echoing his shrill cry. The poor bird, after making one or two steep circuits of the lake, then flew away far out of sight still keeping possession of the fish. He probably went to look for the female at some known and frequented haunt as he flew rapidly off in a direct line. He soon however came over the lake again, and he continued his flight to and fro for about an hour, still keeping the fish ready for his mate. I at length heard the voices of my friends, and we launched the boat. The osprey became much agitated as we neared the rock where the nest was, and dropped the fish he held into the water. We found two beautiful eggs in the nest, of a roundish shape, the colour white with numerous spots and marks of a fine rich red brown. As we came away we still observed the male bird unceasingly calling and seeking for his hen. I was really sorry I had shot her.'

Later that same year he was after them again, near Rhiconnich. St John said that an old woman told them ospreys nested on a loch 'within two or three miles off'; this must have been Loch na Claise Carnaigh on the east side of the village. There they found another nest, built again on a rock out in the loch, and his companion, Dunbar, swam out to it and came back with a young bird and a single egg in his bonnet, which he held between his teeth. To their great chagrin they failed to shoot either of the parent birds, but they soon got wind of another loch to the north-west of Rhiconnich which they apparently had some difficulty in finding. This must have been Loch Mor Chraisg which lies up among the mountains; there are numerous small lochans in the district, it is difficult to say. Here they were more successful. Dunbar again swam to the rock and brought back three young birds. St John shot the male bird in cold blood as it sat on a rock below him watching Dunbar. Even this senseless slaughter had not satisfied him. He returned later that year with Dunbar to the nesting sites he had visited earlier and found, in one case, that the male bird had another mate, and that they were nesting. This nest was again robbed by Dunbar who took the eggs.

In these more enlightened times it is difficult to read these descriptions of the slaughter of a rare and beautiful bird without a feeling of disgust and anger. But it must be remembered that it was not until half a century later that the 'collector-naturalists' put aside the gun. During the first part of this century, localities which rare birds visited on migration, such as Cley in Norfolk, were great hunting grounds for the knickerbockered gentry whose greatest joy was to shoot something uncommon 'to put in a glass case'. Once a bird became rare, then everyone was after it and Charles St John was only doing what others would have done. No doubt to be able to boast you had shot an osprey, or taken its eggs, marked you out as a fine naturalist and a man of note.

At the same time, there still exist today men who have no compunction in robbing a nest if they can add a rare egg to their collection. In the summer of 1958 ospreys returned to an ancient stronghold in the Highlands. Watch was kept upon the nest night and day. But the watch was not good enough. Under cover of darkness a bold rogue managed to reach the island undetected, climbed to the nest and took the eggs. An alarm was raised, he was disturbed, and in getting hurriedly down the tree the eggs were broken. The raider, I am sorry to say, got away.

During the late summer of 1956 I was in the western Highlands on a fishing holiday, and one afternoon I visited a remote and large loch with many islands in it on which grew Scotch firs. I had my telescope with me and, there being no fish moving, I settled down to spy the water. Before I had even raised the telescope, my eye caught two white spots at the crest of one of the dark fir trees on a small island some eight hundred yards away. When I looked

Osprey

through my glass I was amazed (and delighted) to see a pair of ospreys, sitting on a dead branch of pine, one slightly lower than the other. They had evidently been fishing in the loch and were no doubt digesting their meal.

I could see them very clearly, with their fine, noble, crested heads and slender shapes. This loch was, in the past, one of the traditional breeding grounds, perhaps even St John had raided it during his 'summer tour'. It is just possible these birds may have nested there in 1956 for it was a remote spot and it may well have been the pair whose eggs were taken in 1958 in another locality, not so far, 'as the osprey flies', from where I saw my birds.

These, and a spoonbill I saw in Norfolk in September 1958, are the rarest visitors to our shores which I have been lucky enough to see.

* * *

That Sabbath day, when we took the road for Laxford Bridge, was soft and gentle. At times the sun gleamed upon the golden machair and lit the distant mountain peaks. We were amused to see by every crofting the shepherd dogs enjoying their holiday, some lying among the heather or chasing each other round and having great games. Near the head of Shin (it is an immense loch, nearly eighteen miles long), I saw a hoodie crow chasing a peregrine falcon. The falcon was enjoying the game hugely, allowing the furious hoodie to get almost on his tail then doing a backward loop and coming up above the old crow. The battle went on for some minutes and eventually the hoodie retired exhausted and hunched himself on the dead branch of a bog oak growing close to a little burn, where scarlet rowans made a lovely splash of colour. Strange to say, this was the only peregrine I saw on the entire trip but buzzards were plentiful. For some reason, these handsome birds delight in perching on the top of telegraph poles, and many times we stopped the Landrover just below them and they seemed quite tame. I even managed to get a photograph at a few yards' range.

Myxomatosis must have swept the Highlands for I saw very

few rabbits and those were much farther south. When, before the war, I made a camping trip with a tent all round the coast from John O'Groats to Ullapool, I saw some hillsides alive with them. Though the buzzards' diet consisted largely of young rabbits, they have a varied fare, and certainly in some parts of Sutherland they seemed almost as common as hoodies. Though they do take grouse poults, they subsist largely on beetles, and they also eat numbers of grasshoppers, moles, and mice.

The narrow road to Laxford Bridge, where another hooks left for the Kylesku ferry, is delightfully wild and lovely, with the lochs immediately on the right hand and huge shaggy hills on the left, thickly clothed with trees and bracken, with here and there foaming waterfalls tumbling down under the road to the lochs the other side.

There were no deer visible that morning on the high tops by the Duke of Westminster's shooting-lodge; no doubt the violent storms had driven them into the hinterland.

At Laxford Bridge the weather deteriorated still further. The sky was lowering, the rain fell fast. There were two possible camping sites just here close to the bridge, but the 'run in' was from the Durness direction and we could not unhitch and turn the van because of the rain and wind which fell upon us with redoubled fury. The best pitch of all, a stony track which led down to the very margin of a sea inlet, was barred to cars and vans by stakes, a madly irritating thing to travelling van people like ourselves. I had noticed all the way up, from the Border onwards, it was only where landowners and lairds had property bordering the road that these baulks and 'no camping' notices appeared. Perhaps it is that in the holiday season there is annoyance from trippers, and from caravanners who do not know how to leave a pitch clean and tidy, or maybe from roaming tinker bands who always make a camping place into a pigsty.

So we went on, climbing over the high ground through grim mountain scenery bereft of trees, to the high passes above Durness. Here trees vanished completely; in their place enormous blocks of grey golden-sealed granite, larger than a four-storied house, rose from the heather, and small wan lochans shone among the red-gold peat hags.

The curious feature about these high tops are the massive boulders which appear poised along the skylines; seen from a distance they might be helmets of alert men-at-arms peering down into the wild glens. They give one the uncanny feeling of being watched, it is easy to imagine kelpies and trolls dwelling in these rocky places.

In the fifty-six miles from Lairg to Durness we had only passed two cars. I remember when I travelled that road in the early thirties we never saw a car, or even a human being, all the way from Tongue to Durness, and from there to Laxford Bridge, where we met a party of tinkers. Things have changed now. Nearly all the length of the road was well metalled and, though narrow, there are ample passing places.

One curious thing that I must mention is that not once since the beginning of the trip had I seen a hare. This, in the wilds of Scotland, seems astonishing. There were no signs of hare carcasses on the roads. Can it be that this animal is more scarce than it used to be?

Soon we were gliding down the long decline to the Kyles of Durness. Miraculously the clouds vanished eastwards. I drew back Winston's side window and a balmy air met us, and for a moment or so it was easy to imagine it was June. The sun shone golden upon the sides of the moors and gleamed upon the sea lochs which were vivid blue and vitreous green; we even talked of bathing costumes and the prospect of a swim!

We reached the village of Durness (Norse: *Dyranes*, which means 'wild animal headland') around midday and turned the van there before the weatherbeaten Inn, where St John stayed in 1848. This was our northernmost point, for we could go no further in that direction. Eastwards rose the incredibly wild and grim granite cliffs towards Tongue and we glimpsed an inhospitable treeless land; I remembered this stretch of road from my earlier journey and we felt no desire to camp in, or even to explore, the county of Caithness, which is perhaps the most featureless part of this ultimate land.

Everything in the village had a dead and deserted appearance, and though we would have liked to have a drink in the hotel we turned back along the road towards Laxford Bridge. As we went a mass of inky cloud showed over the grim mountains to our right, promising another storm, though as we sped down the road the sun was still shining. I had noticed on our way along this stretch beside the sea loch a level hard place near a little bridge which spanned a burn. Hard by was a delightful sandy bay with the brown burn purling into the tide under the grey stone arches.

On to this level spot we backed the van and had hardly done so when the wind and rain fell upon us with a fury which was almost alarming. The van legs were quickly wound down, Winston was unhitched, and I drove him on the windward side to keep off the violence of the storm which now broke upon us with full force. We tumbled into shelter after first connecting the gas pipe to our container and in a trice we were in the dry once more.

Outside the sky was inky black and the rain beat upon the van like small shot, streaming down the windows in torrents. We were so warm and dry in Romeo we might have been in a luxurious lounge. Within twenty minutes the black wet fury had rushed away from us to the east blotting out the mountains, and everywhere was once again bathed in sunlight, ruddy and warm. I went down to the little bay and walked along the sands.

Life seemed very good that evening as I watched the little ringed plover busy on the shore, hunting among the sea wrack. Their colours, delicate greys and browns, harmonized so well with their surroundings it was hard to see them until they moved. They have an absurd little tittupping run, the legs twinkling. All the plovers have this gait.

There was no worry about where we should go next; as we had no fixed time-table, we could wander where we wished in this lovely land, by the grey Atlantic sea and its white sands, or among the deep glens. I felt as I used to feel as a boy at the beginning of the long vac.

There was something about the smell of the wind as it blew across the Kyle of Durness from the grandly rugged mountains to the west, many over a thousand feet high; there was a sense of adventure, of promise of the good days to come, and the 'not knowing' where we should wander or with what adventures we should meet.

Darkness came quickly and with it wind and menacing clouds. But the rain held off and soon the moon was up, shining eerily on the wet road which led back towards Laxford Bridge. I walked the shore for a mile and struck back over the moor. Rough going it was among the peat hags and I had no torch. Soon I saw before me the cosy glow of the little van on the distant brae by the bridge. Delicious smells of fried onions and cooking steak made me hasten my steps.

* * *

The blue and silver trout spinner which I had bought in Beauly had not so far been tried out, nor had the new and costly thread-line reel which I had bought from home. This was a beauty, and awaited its baptism in its impressive box, hedged round with spare spools and horribly expensive line.

The westering sun: Loch Shin

I must confess at once that I do not pretend to be a skilful fisherman, I am more handy with the gun in the field of sport, but there are occasions when the urge to feel a fighting fish on the end of my cast is not to be denied, and it seemed to me it was high time my spinner and my reel were given an airing.

There was a smallish lochan in the vicinity of our camp (I would prefer not to be more precise) where one day I chanced to wander in the early evening. It lay among sodden acres which smelt of bog myrtle, and was screened by massive golden-sealed boulders. The first time I saw it I felt that here was the place I must bring my rod! At one end was a narrow neck where the shores on either hand approached each other; it was, I suppose, some eighty yards across the open water, just there, and beyond the loch opened out again.

The surface was like glass that evening and as I came over the hill some mallard rose from the slender reeds along the margin by 'the neck'.

I sat down on a rock with my spy glass hoping to see a deer, or perhaps an eagle, when my attention was drawn to the movement of fish in the narrow neck; they were rising every moment, the dimpling rings were continuous. What size they were I could not guess, perhaps the expert could have done so, but I had never seen a rise like this since years ago in Austria, when I was fishing the river Traun. These fish were mad for food and here was I without a rod! Tomorrow evening I would come, just at this time. Perhaps it was a private water; indeed, at the far end, a faded blue boat was drawn up on the shore, bottom up. But no matter, the season was practically at an end. Perhaps the lucky people who owned this ground had gone south in search of other lesser joys and the lodge was empty. Another thing that gave me slight cause for uneasiness was a couple of shooting ponies browsing on the far hill. There was just that faint suspicion of its being preserved ground which was vaguely disturbing. But when I saw those fish rising I knew I must come again!

CHAPTER SEVEN

The Hill Loch

THE following evening found me topping the hill above the loch. I was glad to see the place lay deserted, the ponies had disappeared, and even the ducks were absent. (Though I'm a good enough poacher to know that that, in itself, was not a good sign!)

I lay down among the golden grass and spied the land with my telescope. Nothing but a couple of hoodies across the loch strutting importantly about on the stones!

In front of me tumbled rocks crowned the skyline and a little burn, with a stunted mountain ash leaning over it, made a happy little song to itself close by. Overhead the sky was calm, clear and green, but to the west over Sandwood Bay grey clouds with whitish grey tumbled heads lay along the rugged hills like feather boas.

It was very, very still, only just that little secret talk of the burnlet which was almost invisible amongst its golden grass and stones. I took my light spinning rod out of its bag, a little beauty built for me by that redoubtable angler Richard Walker, who has made such a name for himself as a catcher of coarse fish and, indeed, of trout too. He is the man who caught the record carp from Redmire pool in the West Country, a fabulous giant of forty-four pounds which was hooked and landed in the pitch darkness of a September night.

The gleaming reel came out of its so new box, the line was threaded through the rings, then I was ready.

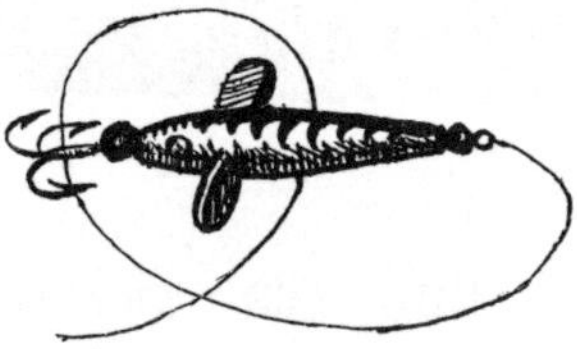

The still peaty-brown water in the neck was ringed again with rising fish though not perhaps so urgently as on the evening before. I drew some line off the spool, nicked up the pick-up, and the little blue and silver spinner described a gentle arc, to fall with a faint plop, no louder than that made by a rising fish, far out in the middle of the neck.

I began to wind in and delighted in the smooth action of the reel, so beautifully geared as to be soundless. Almost at once I felt a fierce 'jag-jagging' on my spinner. This fish did a surprising thing, it made one big rush to my right, charging in among the slender reeds, with quite an impressive bow wave. I have often had a big carp do this when they feel the hook, and sometimes they come right into one's feet and bump their big coarse noses on the bank.

This trout almost beached himself; his black satiny back was twisting among the reed stems, pushing them about, and I had

The autumn road

some difficulty in getting the net under him. A moment later I carried him up the shore among the stones, a beauty of about a pound and three quarters, very dark in colour, peat black on the back, but with an almost tench-like golden hue on his flanks, which were heavily spotted as were the gill covers on his small head. I knocked him over 'the napper' and tucked him under a heather clump. Out went the spinner a second time. Three or four more casts and I was into another. This fish rushed off at an angle, to the right, for the upper part of the loch, the little rod describing a most satisfying arc. With a fixed spool reel even a large trout should not break you if your tackle is sound and the bottom is free from snags. It was clear water out in front but on my right there were some ugly-looking stems (I think they were heather stems) which protruded from the loch, and I had to hold my fish away from these.

A minute or so of stern fighting, during which it leapt out of the water, twice, like a sea trout, and I towed it over the net ring and deposited it on the stones, a fish as like the other as two peas in shape, colour and weight.

After my sixth fish, which I caught with my fourteenth cast, I began to feel a sense of guilt. This was too easy, sheer murder! Five of them were all alike, the last was slightly smaller, a fish of about a pound. Any desirable sporting objective attained without effort becomes undesirable and the more leisure one has the more difficult one likes one's sport to be; which led Robert Gibbings to remark, very wisely (when comparing the monied, leisured fisherman with the poor man poaching), 'There must always be a difference of opinion between those who work all day for a few shillings and those who have so much leisure that they have to invent difficulties to make their fishing less effective.'

Out went the spinner again. This was a pretty cast; the spinner sailed away thirty yards, for the far shore. This time, as I gently wound in, something really big raced off with it, again to the right (most of the fish I hooked seemed to head that way).

I knew I was into a beauty. I played him as carefully as I knew how and he was beginning to come in when he suddenly dashed straight into the protruding stems and was immovable. I tried hand-lining and 'pumping' but the line seemed fast as though I was into the bottom. Eventually, when I was trying a side pull, the spinner suddenly came free in that maddening way they do, and I knew I had lost my best fish. There was a lull then, perhaps the battle had scared the fish away.

I moved down the shore to my right where there was a large flat rock on which I stood. The water seemed pretty deep fairly close in, and I could see the stones shelving steeply down.

I suppose I was greedy. I should have packed up then and been satisfied; after all, I'd caught all we could eat and more. I thought I would make one more cast and hoped it would be a good one. I made it. There was a louder plop ten yards out. I sensed something had gone wrong. It had. The complete spool had come off the casing, I'd never tightened the holding nut securely! This was lying at my feet on the rock, while half my reel and *all* my line, *and* spinner, were out in front of me in the deep water. Mercifully the line had not broken, it was still through the rings.

I was dazed with horror for this was my new reel, remember, and though I had a spare spool, there was no line on it. I can't remember what I paid for that line but it was costly.

I gingerly held the line and began to pull. I went on pulling and the glistening coils began to rise behind me. I had a hundred yards on that reel; it was soon all behind me in a pile half-seen in the fast gathering shadows, like a ball of candy floss. Then I felt the gentle tug of the reel. It was coming along the bottom of the loch! Now and then it would catch on a stone but it came right in. I just couldn't believe it. I pulled it right to my feet, up the spotted stones, and pounced on it.

I just dared not look at the pile of tangled line. I laid the rod down on the rock and went across to the heather bank and collected my fish. Already their lustre was fading and they looked as black and dull as coarse fish. I strung a rush through their gills and made a loop (I hadn't even brought a creel with me), and then went back to my rod, which I took down, and put in the rod bag. Then I rolled up the hideous tangle and pushed it into my pocket.

Just as I turned to go I glanced down the loch to where the beached boat lay among the stones. I saw a man was there beside it, calmly watching me. He had a deerstalker on his head and a crummock in his right hand. He was very tall, but I couldn't see his face for he was too far off; he stood like a fishing heron, just looking at me. A black retriever stood behind him with ears cocked. I did the only thing possible, I pretended not to have seen him. I turned and went up the hill never looking back, my face burning and my ears tingling. But he never shouted. When I got to the top of the brae he was still there, behind the blue boat, just standing, staring at me. So was the dog. I wondered if they had been watching me all the time.

* * *

I had a long walk back to the road and it was rough going. Once I nearly lost my way for the clouds were heavy and it was almost dark, but soon I saw the lights of the van.

I had the feeling that the sooner we ate those trout the better. I cleaned them out and Cecily soon had them in the pan. I was half-expecting a knock on the van door but none came. It took us two evenings to untangle the line. Cecily did it all, working with the utmost patience.

CHAPTER EIGHT

Turbulent Stack, Land of Storms

WE stopped close to Laxford Bridge where a yellow AA box reminds one of civilization and the South.

This prince of rivers, which connects the Duke of Westminster's loch with the sea, is one of the shortest and choicest fishing rivers in the whole of Scotland. I stood on the bridge watching the tumbling waters rushing to the bay beyond and wondered what weight of salmon and sea trout passed up this short stretch in a year. I recalled that Charles St John passed this way in the summer of 1848 on his way to harry the ospreys. He says:

> 'In the course of our drive we passed over a fine-looking stream, the Laxford. Thinking to catch a couple of trout for breakfast, I put my rod together, and leaving the horse and boat standing by the roadside, I determined to take a quarter of an hour's fishing, and if the trout did not rise, to continue

my journey. At the very first cast that I made, however, a large salmon took the fly, rather to my annoyance, knowing as I did that no salmon were allowed to be killed on the Sutherland rivers this season. But being once hooked he might as well be killed, so the fight commenced by the fish running clear out of the stream in which he was first hooked, and going down like a stone to the bottom of a black-looking pool below. Having only a single line and trout tackle, I could not force him much, but after waiting patiently with a gentle but constant strain on the fish, in order that he might feel some weight upon his jaws, I at last, in despair, gave him such a tug that he was dislodged from his resting place in spite of himself. Off he went, sometimes across the stream with nearly my whole line out, the next moment under my feet in the deep pool under the rock on which I was standing, and from which he was not easy to move. There I could see him shaking his head, and trying to rub the hook out against the gravel. At another time he would take a sudden dart to the right and left, and again shake his head, like a dog worrying a rat. But knowing that he was well-hooked, and indeed not caring much whether I lost him or not, I kept so tight a rein on him as prevented him either slacking the line or rubbing off the hook, small as it was.

'Suddenly a new idea seemed to seize him, and shooting straight upwards, he leapt several times out of the water immediately below me.

'But this would not do; so finding he could not get rid of the hook he again rushed across the river, making the handle of the reel spin at railway pace. He then made down stream as fast as he could, I had scarcely any line left on my reel so had to leap off the rock and follow him along the bank of the river. Presently he came to a rather rapid but not high fall, full of broken stones, and altogether a place where he would be sure to break my line if he once got into it, which he seemed determined to do, so here I halted and made a stand against his pulling. The fish began to feel beat, and ran in again almost to my feet.

'Not succeeding in slacking the line, he again rushed right across and took the fall, in spite of all I could do to prevent him. He did not cut my line as I expected, but it gave way close to the end within a few inches of the reel and before I could catch hold of it I had the pleasure of seeing the line floating away, but gradually sinking as the fish carried it off towards the wider pools near the sea.

'Dunbar jumped gallantly into the water, but was too late to catch it, so the salmon went off with about forty yards of line and a couple of sea trout flies in his mouth. I scarcely knew whether to be angry or amused, but considering that the former would be of no use, and perhaps spoil my appetite for breakfast, I undid my rod, got into the boat, and drove off to Scourie to breakfast with a philosophy which rather astonished my companion.'

I must explain that St John, when he describes 'getting into the boat' had invented a novel way of exploring the then almost inaccessible parts of Sutherland. He had built a flat-bottomed boat made of larch and mounted it on wheels. It was constructed to unship in half a minute and by unscrewing a bolt it could be taken off its wheels and launched into the water. He says 'being on springs, it made a very easy carriage, and was large enough to hold four persons with plenty of space for baggage'. It was in this contraption he and Dunbar travelled for many miles, and the boat no doubt came in very handy when he was after the ospreys; perhaps it was originally designed with that in mind.

I shudder to think what would happen to anyone these days if they had the temerity to 'set up his rod' at Laxford Bridge and began to fish the Laxford which is, I believe, one of the most exclusive rivers in Britain. I was told there are five or six 'watchers' on this ground. I expect they are needed.

* * *

We made our camp along the whins on the shores of Loch Stack. There was a level ribbon of greensward where we could pull well off the road, a little burn close by our back door, and a most pleasing view of the reedy grey waters where a little fleet of

Loch Stack

painted widgeon bobbed on the ripples, and grey herons fished at all hours of the day.

The whins gave us snug shelter, thick old bushes which in themselves were primitive houses, for I noticed some wandering tinker had made himself a little room in the heart of one of them. There was the blackened circle of his fire and some empty herring-roe tins.

Behind us was Ben Stack, though we never saw his head for the days were now cold and stormy with much rain, fierce winds, and low cloud.

All day and every day great salmon and sea trout were leaping opposite our windows, sending plumes of spray high in the air like those made by plunging shells. The first night we had hardly finished supper and got into bed when above the wind I heard the grunting and roaring of stags, which went on all night. During the day too, that sound was always present, but never in daylight did they venture near our camp. We heard them roaring on the dark crags above us as we walked the beautiful road which leads to the Overscaig Inn, that Mecca of fishermen, which is renowned for its good sport. As soon as darkness shut down it was a different matter; the stags drew close, as lions roar by camp at night. Heard on the wind their belling had an almost banshee quality.

All this country close to the sea is 'fey', it has a sort of *Mary Rose* feel about it. Not so far distant, no more than thirty miles, are the haunted shores of Sandwood which Seton Gordon describes as the most beautiful place on all the Scottish mainland. An old man, Alexander Gunn of Kinlochbervie, once saw a mermaid there on 5 January 1900. In Macdonald Robertson's fascinating book, *Wade the River—Drift the Loch*, the author tells Gunn's story exactly as it was told to him (in Gaelic) in June 1939. With the author's permission, here it is:

> 'On 5 January (Old Christmas Night) 1900, I was going round after sheep between Sheigra and Sandwood loch. While walking along the edge of the rocky headlands I noticed one of my sheep had fallen down a gully about three miles south-west of Sandwood Bay, known as Ruadh an Fhir

Leithe; and as it was low tide, I descended the cliff towards the sea shore to take it up.

'When I reached the bottom, my collie dog suddenly let out an agonized howl as it crouched in terror close into my feet for protection, with hair bristling, ears set back, and tail between his legs. I looked up. What I saw was so sudden and unexpected that it took my breath away, for, to my astonishment, I observed right above me, what I at first took to be a human being reclining on a ledge of rock only about six or seven feet from where I stood. Then I realized it was a mermaid!

'So impressed was I that I can to this day distinctly recall her appearance, which left a vivid picture on my mind which I can never forget, old man as I am.

'She was no grey seal, she was a mermaid, a bonnie lassie, clear in complexion as ever I saw. Her hair was reddish yellow in colour and curly, and she had a wreath of seaweed round her neck. She had greenish-blue eyes and arched eyebrows and she stared at me with a kind of frightened expression on her face. I remember her appearance distinctly, she had a dark yellowish body, the colour of the yellow tangle on the sea shore.

'Like myself she got a fright. She never moved, not even her wee short arms, as she reclined amidst the noise of the surf with her fish-like tail dangling over the other side of the rock. She did not speak. I sensed the situation right away: she could not move until the high tide came! She was marooned upon the rock on which she rested! She was in angry mood, angry that I had discovered her, and she was frightened too.

'It was all very difficult to describe, but she was the size of an ordinary human being, with the same features, but she had an arched back. She was very beautiful, ravishingly so.

'For minutes only the mermaid and I gazed at each other, then realizing that what I saw was supernormal, I took to my heels in terror. What I had seen, coupled with the remembrance of my dog's howls on reaching the shore, frightened me and I must confess, I followed after my dog in trembling fear of the maiden of the sea.'

Perhaps it was the same mermaid (or her sister) which was seen by a lady who was fishing from a rowing-boat on Loch Inchard on 24 June 1939. She suddenly saw, floating on the water, what she took to be a bunch of yellow seaweed. To her utter astonishment it turned about in the water revealing a beautiful girl's face with blue eyes and delicate colouring. Then with a splash of her big tail she was gone.

Loch Inchard is only three miles from where Alexander Gunn saw his mermaid thirty-nine years before, and I imagine mermaids never grow old. Note that both mermaids had the same-coloured hair, the colour of the sea tangle.

* * *

I was thinking of Alexander Gunn's strange story that first night by Stack, as I lay listening to the faint roaring of the stags and the beat of the waves out in the loch. I remembered, too, a most eerie experience of my own which happened before the war, when my cousin and I, with a little tent, pitched camp on a mountain side beyond Badcall, not six miles from the very spot where Gunn saw his mermaid.

Darkness had overtaken us on the road and it was with some difficulty that we found a moderately sheltered spot on the hillside among the rocks and heather. Our tent had a fly-sheet under which we placed a box containing our provisions, our pots, mugs, and plates.

The wind came howling from the sea, buffeting our frail tent, and the night was intensely black though fine. I was just dropping off to sleep when I heard distinctly the sound of padding feet around the tent. I lay listening for a while to these mysterious noises and at last awoke Jock who heard them too. Then there was the sound of metal clinking on china from the store box.

I flashed on my torch and poked my head under the edge of the tent. I saw nothing, but something rushed off into the darkness. We were both feeling very scared and I drew the box into the tent with us, putting it by my feet. Then I switched off the torch and we lay again listening. The wind had died away, only occasional gusts shook the tent, and we could hear the unearthly laughter of loons down on the big loch close to the road—a hideous sound to hear at the dead of night, or indeed at any time.

We were just sinking to sleep again when I heard the same dread footsteps once again. There was no snuffling or breathing but the same muffled padding. I waited trembling in my blanket bag with my torch ready and my hunting knife drawn from its sheath.

The next moment I leapt up in terror for I felt the wooden box being drawn bodily out of the tent. Whatever creature it was had come in under the edge of the canvas and had seized hold of the box. I flashed on the light.

The box was resting on the grass right side up, half-pulled out under the canvas wall, and it was being tugged viciously by something outside. With a wild yell, as bloodcurling as the noise made by the loons, I tumbled out of the tent. I was too late to see what our nocturnal visitor was. There was a rushing and a scurrying among the rocks and heather, the clink of stones sent rolling, and it had gone.

We spent the rest of the night with a candle burning between us. Neither of us slept a wink.

This midnight raider may well have been a wild cat, for they abound in the district, but a cat, tame or wild, is a silent-footed creature and these footsteps sounded uncommonly like human, or shall I say supernatural ones!

* * *

On this, our first night at Stack, when the roaring of the stags was about us, some of them must have been on the road, and it was there that I had the encounter with the old grey stag below Ben Stack, described in the first chapter.

The following night they were all around us again. One was making such a noise it roused the Peke who sat up shivering with tail depressed and large goggling eyes showing the whites. I had a very powerful electric torch which threw a vivid beam and creeping to the door of the van I opened it and shone the light on to the little boggy shore below, which lay between us and the water. There, within thirty yards of us, was a big beast facing us. The light from the torch made his eyes appear huge and pink which gave him a most uncanny ghoulish appearance. For some moments he stood thus with ears wide, fixing his gaze on us, then wheeling round, he splashed away through the bog.

* * *

We were weather-bound among the whins for several days. The rain fell in torrents, and a sombre gloom covered the landscape; in all our time there we barely glimpsed the sun. Eventually we moved on towards Lairg, and as we travelled along the road by Shin, we saw afar off the first sun for days, bathing Lairg and the golden country beyond so that it looked like a promised land.

Yet despite the foul and gloomy weather (a raven flew over us as we pulled out, croaking hoarsely) I was sorry to leave that wild country. The memories of it even now are more insistent than those of the golden glens Garry and Affric, which were to be our next camping grounds.

CHAPTER NINE

South to Strath Glass

WHAT a joy it was to see the sunlight once more, gilding the heather, flashing on the streams! It was as if we had been imprisoned in a dark cell for weeks, with no sounds but the roaring of the winds and stags, the guttural croaks of ravens, the continuous drip of rain.

Now, upon this clear autumn morning, we were once again upon the road to Bonar Bridge, with its blue waters and herds of white whoopers, and the drooping golden birch trees carpeting the roads before us with their heart-shaped amber leaves.

When we were some miles short of the village, passing through a little 'drogue' of birch, we saw in front of us, right in the centre of the road, a diminutive figure coming our way. For some moments I could not identify this pilgrim; it looked like a small rabbit at first, then I thought, as it came closer, it was a rat. At last I saw it was a hedgehog about six weeks old, its spines still soft, and with a most disturbed expression in its grave little eyes (the eyes of a hedgehog are as wise as those of an elephant).

'What a darling!' exclaimed Cecily, 'but what's he doing in the road?'

I brought Winston to a halt, got out, and lifted the hedgehog up.

'I don't think he's too well,' I said. The little animal did not seem to be unduly alarmed and made little effort to curl up, which was a bad sign. When I put him on my lap, and gently pressed his forehead prickles, he unrolled completely. I have a 'way' with hedgehogs and they understand me, but this one seemed unusually insensitive. I had noticed over the last few days numberless carcasses of young hedgehogs flattened on the mountain roads, especially in those places where bracken fringed the sides and woods came close. Perhaps they were looking for their winter hibernation quarters for in late autumn they become restless. I was aware, too, that we had had some hard frosts of late, and now the frost had gone and the sun shone warmly the hedgehogs had, no doubt, re-emerged, like wasps and flies do on a warm day in late autumn. Usually when this takes place it bodes ill for them for this sun of late October is treacherous, temperatures can drop in a matter of minutes, and hard frosts may strike suddenly at night.

'What shall we do with him?' asked Cecily, stroking his head prickles. 'Take him along with us,' I said. 'We'll fix up a box for him when we get to Bonar Bridge. I'll get him some bracken, and he'll be as snug as a flea under a dog's ear.' So I tucked him inside my coat where he crawled against my left side and lay still, in the warm and the dark.

Ping's round head appeared over my shoulder. Little silver bubbles decorated the ends of her whiskers. She could smell the newcomer and was determined to investigate. Hedgehogs must possess a most appetizing smell for dogs, for it seems to drive them frantic. Possibly they smell of tender pork; no doubt they taste very like it too.

Many times I have wanted to taste hedgehog and have even caught one, intending to devour it. My heart has always quailed at the thought of administering the *coup de grâce*. In any case, I don't know how one would kill a hedgehog humanely.

We stopped at an hotel in the sunny main street of Bonar Bridge, and when I was drinking my inferior Scotch beer, I took Bonny out of my coat (of course he had to be called Bonny) and set him running on the bar-top, to the amusement of the customers and of the landlady who served us. A box was speedily produced, an old Huntley and Palmer's biscuit tin, and he was put inside and covered liberally with red bracken which was rustling and dry.

* * *

Instead of following the coast road round the firths to Beauly, we turned right by the loch of the wild swans (they were there in force, brilliantly white against the blue water) and crossed over to the Cromarty Firth by that magnificent road over the mountains. There below was spread out an impressive panorama of the firth, vivid blue in the morning sun, with all the folded hills marching down to it gold, red, and green. We rejoined our original road half-way along the Cromarty Firth. A seal was out on the tide edge, a few whooper swans, and countless ducks and waders. I would have liked to camp in the only place available on its shore, a stony lay-by under the arch of a bridge, but a huge red lorry was taking its siesta there, and there was not room for us all. Moreover the road was busy with rushing traffic. So we went on through Beauly and took the road which runs up to Strath Glass beside the Beauly river.

Up the glen we came upon a wide space on the left of the road by a trestle bridge. There was a delightful jungle of alders, hazel, and birch just there and it was sheltered.

We had had wretched wakeful nights with the storms by Stack and were glad to find this quiet haven, where robins sang their sorrowful autumn songs, and a fine red squirrel was feeding on the hazel nuts. These delightful little creatures, which we never see at home, are still common in parts of Scotland. I stood underneath a hazel bush and the tiny animal skipped in the boughs above, with a nut in its mouth, looking down at me.

We brought Bonny in from the Landrover and put him on the table where he soon ran about and ate some bread and milk with much relish. He made as much noise over this as a bearded old man drinking soup. Ping, who was asleep at the other end of the van, suspected that I was kissing Cecily. She rose up in wrath to come and separate us and had to be restrained. Hedgehogs are always noisy eaters. Later, when they grow old, they are inclined to be asthmatical. I have often heard one wheezing and coughing in the summer evenings, when they have been hunting in the garden for worms and beetles. Once they get tame and used to being handled, they never roll up. Contrary to popular belief, hedgehogs can move fast, at a brisk trot. When in rapid motion they give one the impression of running on casters for there is no rocking motion. Like some people I know, hedgehogs are 'no good in the mornings'.

Having finished his supper, Bonny explored the table-top, licked his chops, and fell off the table on to his nose. He was then returned to his bracken bed in the biscuit tin, where he promptly dropped asleep. Young hedgehogs are delightfully pretty little creatures and Bonny promised to become very friendly and tame.

That evening was calm and tranquil, with the *triste* song of robins from the hazels, typical October, real 'tinker's weather'. The alders about our sheltered camp were as green as in summer, without a brown leaf anywhere; only the hazels and beeches were red and gold, and the bracken its usual rich hue.

* * *

I am certain there can be no more magnificent awe-inspiring river scenery in the whole of the Highlands than this superb valley of the Beauly river and Strath Glass. Turrets and islands of granite divide the stream which flows far below the road in a deep gorge, exactly like an engraving by Dürer. On one massive granite tower, impregnable in mid-stream, small birches grow, their yellow leaves a rare contrast to the dark tones of the rock, and one solitary Scotch fir, sown by some passing bird, perhaps even a cross-bill,

The fantastic beauty of the Beauly River

which perched a moment there. The seed passed through the bird and fell into some moist crevice in the rock which provided sustenance.

This whole rocky gorge, with the peat-brown river swirling deep and dark from pool to pool, is like some fantastic but extremely beautiful illustration to a fairy tale, and I marvel that it is not famed throughout Scotland. It should be as famous as Glencoe, for it is vastly more impressive, and such scenery is rare in Britain. Yet I have never heard it mentioned; I have never seen pictures of it. We stood on the road looking down hundreds of feet at the swirling torrent, and were struck dumb with astonishment and even awe. Perhaps this is the time to see it, when the dark forbidding precipices and rocks throw into vivid relief the pale ambers, golds and yellows of the autumn trees which thickly clothe the steep banks.

Later I learnt to my disgust and dismay that this natural beauty will soon be no more. On the centre turret rock I had seen a notice board with one sinister word DAM. As I thought, the Hydro-electric Scheme is taking this river into its plans and that pillar of rock will, I suppose, serve as a support for the dam which will be thrown across the gorge. The scheme will be completed in about nine years from now, so I was told in Beauly. Already the yellow Wimpey lorries are as busy as nest-building wasps.

Talking of wasps, that evening as I peeled onions before the van door one flew inside and settled on the wardrobe. This was indeed a sign of the change in climate.

Tinkers had camped here, for the hazel thickets had been cut and chips lay about—hazel makes the best clothes pegs. The marks of their fires were old, and maybe they had passed this way in the tourist season.

These strange wild peoples are not so mechanized as are the English gypsies and are altogether more primitive, living in tents, not vans. I remember, years ago, making camp in wild country between Loch Inver and Inchnadamff, in a little birch wood far from the main road. I had pitched my tent and was busy grilling some trout for my supper when I heard the beat of horses' hooves along the track down which I had come. I was not too pleased when I saw a party of tinkers—one old man leading a donkey, which pulled a little tilt cart, and two or three women and a few younger men, all very ragged and wild-looking, tagging along behind. I hoped they would pass by, but after a moment's hesitation and confabulation on the road, during which they eyed me all the time, they moved into the wood not more than a hundred yards distant and took the donkey out of the shafts. The men then busied themselves with sticking long withies into the ground, bending them over into hoops. From the cart they took a large waterproof sheet which was thrown over the hooped sticks. Meanwhile the women had been busy gathering bracken, bringing back armfuls of it to the tent which they packed inside to form a mattress. (I had done the same myself in my own tent. Bracken makes a delightfully elastic bed and is as good as any spring mattress.) They then lit a fire and set supper cooking, chattering like starlings all the while, and now and again swearing volubly, all in Gaelic.

I was not too happy to have such bedfellows so close but there was nothing for it, and I had no intention of moving. So I piled my fire high, and when I had had my supper, I lay beside it, smoking my pipe, and watching the red flames lighting up the silvery stems all around me. After some time I heard a stick crack behind me in the wood and a handsome young gypsy lad, of about sixteen years of age, came out of the darkness. He nodded in a friendly way and sat down beside me by the fire, talking in Gaelic (which I could not of course understand). Our conversation was therefore limited, to say the least, but he seemed quite content to stay with me and helped me to break sticks for the fire.

At last he got up, nodded again in a friendly way, and went back to his own people. But as soon as he rejoined them there was an outburst of angry shouts and talking in raised voices. Eventually the old man, who seemed the patriarch of the tribe, took up a big stick, and seizing the boy by the collar, gave him a most terrible thrashing. The noise was indescribable, like a pack of jackals fighting, with the men swearing and the ladies joining in with high-pitched screams. It was some time before all was quiet and I saw their fire slowly die to ash. I cannot say I spent a very easy night but when I awoke next morning they had gone and none of my gear was missing.

* * *

The next day was a lazy one, enabling Cecily to get some family washing done. We strung a line from the Landrover to the van and hung out our 'smalls' as unashamedly as any old gypsies. In the mellow afternoon light, I went nutting among the hazels by Beauly's banks. I collected a hatful, though the nuts were very difficult to see among the yellowing foliage. As I pushed about among the rounded leaves, searching for the little polished helmets which so cleverly conceal themselves from all but a squirrel's eyes. W. H. Davies' lines came into my head:

'And the woodnuts rich to make us go
Into the loveliest lanes I know.'

My mind went back to a bright April day, with blue skies and puffed clouds sailing, when I was introduced to the poet in his pleasant garden in Worcestershire.

He struck me at once as an intensely shy man, not altogether happy in his surroundings. He had a quaint manner of looking at you sideways. As he limped round the garden paths, showing me his flowers and his bird-table, he said in his very deep voice, 'D'you know, I've been asked to write a book on my "garden birds" and I know nothing about birds! What am I to do?'

Though I only met him that once I liked him immensely: he reminded me of some shy, rough-haired, bank vole. My uncle, who was a great friend of the poet, used to take him out to dine in London. Davies was terrified of smart 'eating-places' and went in horror of being presented with a menu written in French!

* * *

This day was the sunniest and warmest we had had since we began our autumn journey. The blaze of gold we saw that morning is still in my mind as I write; I never imagined anything could be so lovely.

After tea, when I came back from an abortive attempt to catch a brown trout, we noticed the bracken fronds in Bonny's tin were quivering. We made up his tea, earth-worms and bread and milk, removed him from his tin, placed him on the table and bade him eat. He did not resent being lifted out and set to at once in his usual greedy, noisy, fashion. He filled himself with bread and milk, and devoured three earth-worms, one after the other, with a relish which was both appreciative and noisy. He was much more at home, shaking himself in a dog-like fashion, and depressing his prickles so that he was quite soft to the touch; I noticed he smelled of mossy hedgerows. I never realized that these little animals had such long tails—his was as long as a mole's and much the same shape.

CHAPTER TEN

To the Glen of the Dappled Ford

THERE was a change in the weather next morning, Friday, 24 October. The blue sky had gone, and clouds drifted over. A breeze stirred the birches, sending showers of yellow leaves spinning high into the sky. It was decidedly cooler, but the sun gleamed forth at intervals.

During the night Ping had wakened us, giving Cecily an attack of 'camp asthma'. This curious complaint is very prevalent among those who sleep in the open air, especially those who favour tents. In the small hours there is an atmospheric change which affects the bronchial tubes. I have often suffered with this tiresome complaint myself when sleeping under canvas in my army days. It is akin to the change of temperature in water which sends fish gasping to the top; lack of oxygen or too much of it, nobody can tell me which is the cause.

We noticed that one of Ping's eyes looked rather blue. It was

Sunset over Affric

worrying her, and worried us too, as ever since she was a puppy she had had trouble with both her eyes, mostly caused by ingrowing eyelashes. We had had both her eyelids operated on, very skilfully, by our local vet just before our trip, and we hoped this could cure the trouble.

* * *

I suppose there are other glens as impressive as Affric, and perhaps another year I may make another autumn journey and

explore them. Just then, in late October, I could imagine nothing finer. It was thickly wooded, the bracken was high, the birches bearded with deer moss. Bilberries formed soft hummocks on the low ground (I found some with berries still on them), and everywhere tiny gutters wept downwards through the green draw moss and the hart's-tongue fern. Here no traffic passed. All we heard was the dull boom of the waterfall under the new bridge by our camp.

As with an increasing number of Highland glens, the North of Scotland Hydroelectric Scheme people have thrown a dam across the eastern end of the loch, and we had the same setup at the foot of our brae. The old Highland 'drove' road wound in and out, showing at times in a solitary narrow bend and curve, and appearing from the deep water to dive again into the depths; the same 'drowned road' we found by Shin, 'drowned' as will be the very road we travelled that morning up Strath Glass.

Bonny, the infant hedgehog, seemed too lethargic to eat that night. We got him out of his bracken bed and spread his banquet but his eyes did not open wide and he moved as if in a dream. I imagined that his winter sleep was upon him and that he wished to be left in peace. So we returned him to his bed, covered him up, and left him.

The moon was nearly full, shining serenely on the waters of Loch Beinna a Mheadhoin spread out below us. Looking out of the window we saw its broad glittering silvery path crinkling gently before a soft westerly wind—'a silver path across a silver sea'. It was a picture of awesome majesty, the thick Scotch firs on the island, the black rocks appearing as if cut out of cardboard, and the mountains on the far shore with stars shining brightly above them.

Cecily was soon asleep, breathing gently by my side, and I could hear the diminutive snores of Ping who had retired to the spare bunk in the corner with her circular head laid upon a pillow. From where I lay, wakeful, but at peace, I saw the clear, hard edge of the moon come sidling out into the square of the window until there it was, crisp and detailed, its pallid light full upon me. This sly appearance set me thinking on this 'rainbow planet that is tumbling through a physical universe of inconceivable dimensions', as Llewelyn Powys once described it, and of the various bits of ironmongery we have recently discharged beyond the moon.

That excellent lecturer, Patrick Moore, who delights thousands (and scares a few) on our TV screens, with his dispassionate accounts of the vastness of space, has a knack of giving to the simple man like myself a wonderful idea of the immensity of the universe. He makes the most soul-shattering pronouncements and does not bat a lid of his hypnotic eyes, yet I sometimes feel my reason shrivelling at the thought of the limitless void around us, at the idea of planets and stars, hundreds of times larger than the sun, which cruise around in outer space.

I feel, too, a profound sadness when Patrick Moore reminds us that nothing in the universe can be permanent, that even the sun must one day die; and before it does, so must our own minute globe of matter which, to some of those giants like 'Beetlejuice', is no more than a pebble in size, a mere meteorite.

What purpose, one is forced to wonder, is there then in any effort, in *Hamlet*, the *Venus de Milo*, in the *Mona Lisa*—every great work of art that has ever been wrought by man? What purpose in sacrifice, noble deeds, or endeavour, if all must perish?

I once heard Moore make an apt comparison between the crowd in a busy city street and the planets and stars in the universe. Walking along a thoroughfare, one can see all manner of human beings—infants in arms, toddlers, and so on, to the aged. And he who looks into outer space, with the limited means we have at our disposal, can see planets and stars which are young, old, and aged; one can even see the birth of a star.

There perhaps, lies the hope we yearn for. We know light will not go out of the universe, the mysterious process of rebirth continues, and total darkness and nothingness can never be. The very fact that we can understand these truths and ponder them in our hearts is in itself a hope for the future, and as for the present, I would echo Llewelyn Powys's last testament: 'Live life, live every moment of life that you experience without pain.'

* * *

The moon passed on. Its light dwelt, in ghostly fashion, first upon the window curtains, the wall, the wardrobe, and then was gone; only a single star remained there, framed in the window. Before it reached the right-hand edge I was asleep.

Old birch trees in Glen Affric

CHAPTER ELEVEN

'Skulking in Ye Highlands'

At the head of Loch Beinna a Mheadhoin a road barred to motor traffic winds through a wild and heathery country to the shore of Loch Affric. Ancient Scots firs grow on either hand, reminding one of Victorian oil paintings of the Highlands; you may even see Highland cattle to complete the picture. These firs, I understand, are of immense age, some of the oldest in Scotland. Whether that be true I know not.

That soft grey morning when I walked the road, red grouse were skimming over the heather, buzzards mewed, invisible, disembodied voices, up in the mountain mists, and two large birds (I liked to think they might be golden eagles) wheeled in concentric circles above the heights of Sgurr la Lapaich whose 3,401 feet were crowned with cloud.

In every fir-top fieldfares sat upright, clucking their wild notes, and flirting their grey rumps, whilst flock after flock passed eastwards over the glen.

A spear of silver light pierced the grey face of Affric and was gone, a soft wind sent the painted mountain ash leaves wavering to the banks of the river. I came upon a man in the narrow way. He had a camera on a tripod, trained on the ripples seen through a fretted frame of larch twigs. He was waiting patiently for a gleam of sun to light the scene, waiting as patiently as a fisherman. When I returned he had gone, and I wondered if he had seized the moment of truth.

Why, oh why, do people travel in other lands when there is all this beauty at their very doors?

The vastness of the alpine country of Switzerland and Austria is too theatrical for my tastes; here we have the same beauty in miniature, more personal, less aloof. I wished that every autumn I could wander in all the glens of Scotland. With a sigh I thought of the beauty I could never see, loch, and mountain, moor and forest, many hundreds of square miles which must be, like books unread, forever unknown.

There is ever the stern business of living, of winning one's daily bread, and though luckier than most in my present home environment, I could not but feel envy of those who can wander at any time, anywhere, whilst they are still young in mind and body. I sometimes think (perhaps quite in error) that the majority of people who have 'the means' find other and shallow delights in the cities and the man-made artificial world; all that I hold most valuable is to them something quite apart.

In some places near our encampment huge granite rocks lay tumbled under the ancient lichen-bearded birches, their bases hidden in mounds of blueberry. One block I noticed, shaped like the creased face of a Blakish monster, wore a tufted turban of blueberry.

The grey rocks, some crowned with Scotch firs, would have delighted Arthur Rackham. They are crannied and fissured and sprout ferns and fungi, whilst all round the graceful palm-like bracken fronds form a screen of pinkish orange and deep red, a screen dense enough to hide a hundred kelpies. On the evening of 25 October I heard a solitary owl hooting up in the woods, probably one of the long-eared kind. No red squirrels played about in the trees, even the hoodie crow was absent.

By moonlight these hanging woods up Glen Affric are especially ghostly. Here and there the moonbeams catch on the silvery stem or stump of a birch; one can almost imagine a dimly-lit lantern shining steadily there, mysterious and ghostly.

Bonny remained somnolent in his biscuit tin, covered with bracken; we hardly knew if he was sleeping or dying. From his peevish grunts, however, when we stirred him with our fingers, we thought he was preparing for his winter hibernation.

Most days the winking ripples moved across the surface of the loch from west to east, even though there was apparently no wind, but in the bays sheltered by the islands and rocks the water was like a polished mirror, reflecting every detail of the trees on the far shore. Many of these islands have white sandy beaches, all are grown with dark Scotch firs—a real picture-postcard loch. These islands must be rarely visited by man. Perhaps in the summer season a fisherman lands from his boat and eats his sandwiches among the blueberry bushes, but many must be quite forsaken from one year's end to another.

How I longed for something to watch, a herd of whoopers, even a mallard, or a heron fishing, but nothing moved save the eternal crinkling ripples under the soft autumn sky.

One afternoon, however, I did meet with a little adventure which was rewarding. I was on the other side of the ridge from our camp, in Fasnakyle Forest. Away to the north-west the gleaming length of Loch Mullardoch lay peaceful and unruffled under the soft grey sky, and beyond it the high mountains in Glencannich Forest were veiled in cloud. I was walking among the larches when I heard the voice of a bird I failed to recognize. I flatter myself I know the call notes and songs of most inland British birds. It was a sharp penetrating call and I immediately began to search the tops of the larches about me. I was delighted to see, after a little while, a company of cross-bills, numbering about a dozen or more, all busy in the larch-tops among the cones. There were some fine cock birds among them, with rosy red breast and

The rainbow over Rannoch

head, and a number of dusky juveniles. This red of the cross-bill is not obvious when you see the bird against the sky, when it is like a drab, large-sized sparrow, but against a background of dark fir, its full beauty is apparent. It is not bright like the colour of a cock bullfinch, but more a golden rose, exactly the tint of the 'pincushion' growths which one often sees on wild roses and which is caused by a parasite.

We see the cross-bill very occasionally in the Midlands; indeed, I saw some in Northamptonshire in late December 1958, which was a 'cross-bill year' when many were seen all over the Midland area. But these Highland birds seemed far more colourful and were, I imagine, Scottish variety, which differs slightly from the southern.

I watched them for an hour, hunting along the tree-tops, snipping at the cones with their strange curved, crossed bills which are so well adapted for extracting the seeds from the cones. All the time, one or another would keep up the strange penetrating call which is not unlike the conversational remarks made by the greenfinch but with a greater carrying power.

Cross-bills are early breeders and resemble the raven in this respect. They begin nesting in January and February, but mostly in March. It is difficult to understand why some species who breed in mountain country in the north should choose to nest when the winter is most rigorous. I have never found an explanation for this. Perhaps the food is then most suitable, the seeds of the cones at the right degree of ripeness. Whatever the reason, both parent and young must be very hardy and able to withstand extremes of cold. Their antics among the topmost twigs of the larches reminded me very much of parrots, for they sidle and twist their bodies in the same way.

Glen Cannich, which we explored one afternoon, and which is reached from the village of Cannich at the beginning of Glen Affric, is in some ways more beautiful than the latter. It is narrower, the road is much steeper and more thickly wooded, and in the afternoon light it appeared particularly beautiful.

The westering sun was dipping behind the mountains on our

left, but its ruddy rays lit the mountain tops on the right of the glen, picking out all the trees dressed in their autumn finery. This glen is wilder and less frequented than Affric; possibly because of its narrow twisting road, motor cars were absent.

On a scarlet-berried rowan by the river which flows at the bottom of the glen a buzzard, a bird of the year, sat regarding us.

CHAPTER TWELVE

To Laggan and Glen Garry

It was a serene October morning with no wind, and the leaves falling softly in the glens.

We pulled out, regretfully, from our wonderful site up Affric at about ten o'clock. The waters of the loch were mirror-still, ringed by the rising of innumerable trout. I had in my mind for our next halting place one of the most beautiful lochs in the Highlands, that of Loch An Eilein ninety miles to the east. This gem is unfortunately close to Aviemore—I say 'unfortunately' for any loch near to a tourist centre has its drawbacks, as we shall see.

There is an island in Loch An Eilein (which means in Gaelic 'the loch of the island') and upon it is a squat grim ruin, ivy-clad. Here, up to a comparatively short time ago, ospreys nested, and continued to do so well into this century. Also in Rothiemurchus forest is another of our rarest British birds, though much smaller than the osprey: the crested tit, which is practically confined to this small area.

We journeyed in leisurely fashion back to Inverness, and, joining the main road, we travelled along the shores of the Beauly Firth. The tide was at full flood and on the meagre grassy marsh edge hundreds of waders were massed in the sun, waiting for the tide to drop. A little further out were rafts of widgeon and mallard, floating tight-packed like little painted boats. Here and there a handsome black-backed gull stood apart with his wicked bill and still more wicked eye, plainly visible.

We followed again the rather dreary road for Aviemore and, it being nearly midday, stopped at a wayside hotel for a drink. A man sitting on a seat in the corner, smoking his pipe and with a glass of beer in his hand, seemed very interested in our journey, and when he asked my name he told me he had read all my books. It was flattering, in an out-of-the-way spot in the Highlands, to meet someone who knew my work, and it gave a fillip to my pride.

Soon after, we came to Aviemore (the name in Gaelic means 'the big gap') and beyond it we hooked left under a railway arch and followed a narrow twisting road in search of Loch An Eilein. We came upon it at last 'midst red-leaved beeches and dark firs. To my intense disgust and disappointment we found a large notice board which said NO CAMPING, NO FIRES TO BE LIT.

We left the caravan in the narrow road and hurried across the close-cropped green turf to the shores of this exquisite loch, which has the reputation, and deservedly so, of being the most beautiful of all the Highland lochs. The wind was cold, despite the sun, funnelling straight down at us from the island, and we saw that same ruin upon which the fish eagle used to build.

All around rose the blue mountains, a pearly mist hung over the water which slapped noisily on the little stony beach by the green turf. There was an ideal site for our van, flat and firm, with the romantic island and its ruin in front of us. The ruin itself dates back to Robert the Bruce and belongs (according to Seton Gordon's fascinating book *Highways and Byways in the Central Highlands*, one of my favourite volumes both for the beauty of the writing and the illustrations by Sir D. Y. Cameron) to the family of Grant, who have possessed the lands of Rothiemurchus since the late sixteenth century.

The ruin itself, according to Seton Gordon, was the scene of a grim revenge. A certain Lauchlan Macintosh, chief of his clan, had been murdered by a near kinsman in 1524. The Macintosh clan, enraged at this, pursued the murderers to Loch An Eilein. The three chief culprits were kept in chains in the castle on the island until 1531 when the chief murderer, Malcolm, was beheaded and quartered, and the other two were first tortured and then hanged.

Seeing this somewhat square, sinister-looking little ruin, on its tiny island out in the loch, made me think of those three wretches kept in chains in some narrow dungeon for seven whole years and then executed in some barbarous fashion. No doubt even the dungeon walls could not stifle the screams of those tortured wretches. Those were dark and terrible times when a man's life was held cheap and his existence depended on his keen eye and ear and even keener claymore.

I was completely under the spell of this delightful lake (the loch is no more than a mile long) and felt uneasy anger at not being allowed to rest there and drink in the scene. Yet how right it is, after all, that people should not camp there! What a pigsty it would become with the blackened scars of fires, the empty tins, the bottles, the paper! One can see it all, the work of wretched louts who do not know how to behave in a place such as this. I very soon realized that, if I were a Grant, I too would allow no one to camp there; of *course* it is right, there is no other alternative.

I managed to take a picture of the castle, and its island and the misty peaks beyond. Then we went sorrowfully back to the road where we had to unhitch the caravan to turn it round, coupling it to Winston which was also backed and turned. As we returned along the leafy road I glimpsed a man who looked very like a keeper, with a dog at his heels, hurrying forward through the trees towards the loch. No doubt word had gone forth that a caravan had passed that way and he was hastening to investigate.

It was now well past noon. We had made a wide detour to see

On the road by Loch Laggan

Loch An Eilein, and by rights we should have travelled south by the shores of Loch Ness, towards our next camp place in Glen Garry, so we were tired as we rumbled onwards into the westering sun. We came to Newtonmore, a bright little place, and here we turned right for Loch Laggan, which we reached an hour before sunset. We had done over a hundred miles, and were anxious to find a suitable camping site for the night. This we discovered at the head of the loch, on a wide grassy margin hard by the highway but with a fine foreign-looking view, across the bare sand-bars at the head of the loch, to Ben Alder, home of the wild cat and the eagle.

I can understand now the anxiety that gypsies must feel at the approach of night when they have no settled camping site. Whenever we came upon big 'policies' with pheasants and lodge gates, we felt uneasy and hurried on. Such localities are hostile to the traveller and one feels it. The neatly clipped laurels, the orderly rhododendrons, have a 'keep off, keep out' look! I did see one polite notice that day, however: 'NO CAMPING PLEASE'. So much better than 'NO CAMPING', 'Proceedings will be taken', etc., etc., which we saw so many times during our travels. One notice in Glen Quoich said 'Keep to the Road', without as much as a 'please'.

Talking of pheasants, that morning Cecily saw one in the road in front of us and she put on all speed. The bird went under our wheels but flew on into the wood, cocking as it went. We had missed a good meal, so a rich belly would benefit and a poor belly go lean!

As with many of the Highland waters we had so far seen, Laggan seemed very low, despite the fact that the summer had been wet in Scotland. Looking across the wind-troubled waters, across the dunes and sand-bars and the dark fir woods on the far shore, with the mountains rising behind, I was strongly reminded of Austria. There was no sign of life on the loch, no wildfowl of any sort. Perhaps the reason was that most of these Highland lochs have stony barren shores offering no food for the duck tribe which delight in marshy places and swampy heads to lochs. As evening deepened into dusk a fine sunset flared in the west, with pink airy clouds on a green ground, and tumultuous banks of pearly cloud.

One amusing incident enlivened our rather weary journey from Newtonmore. As I drove I suddenly felt a pricking on my left leg. I thought it must be a sleepy wasp and looked down. Lo and behold, there was Bonny the hedgehog, whom everyone thought had entered upon his long winter sleep! He had been travelling in his tin, covered with bracken, right at the back of the Landrover. During our drive he had somehow climbed out of his tin and, with that remarkable agility which is typical of these spiny hedge pigs, had surmounted piles of boxes, tins, waders, sacks, and I know not what else, and had found his way to my feet! He was obviously hungry, so as soon as we reached our camping site his saucer was brought out, bread and milk put therein, and he set to with a will, eating until his little tummy was full, when he was returned once more to his tin.

For supper that night we had haggis, a favourite dish of mine when in the north. It was tied (before we cooked it) with a tartan ribbon. Cecily remarked how horribly like Bonny it was, Bonny without prickles and wearing an Order. It was certainly the same shape, and exactly the same size!

The following morning was indeed a flawless gem; a warm sun was shining from a sky without cloud, the wide sands of the loch head gleamed with mother of pearl lights, and the distant wooded mountains were lit by tender colours.

At the foot of our brae was a splendid mountain ash full in the sun and heavy with berries. Upon it a handsome mistle thrush came and sat, bolt upright, turning his head, his bold eye apprais-ing God's lovely morning. It filled him with well-being as it did me. Ping, too, stretched out by the open window on top of the seat cushion, basked like a cat before a hearth, eyes closed, paws outstretched like a woolly sphinx. These were surely moments that were not being wasted; these I would remember perhaps when I was old—the brilliant scarlet berries among the clear yellow leaves, the silvery tones of the water reflecting the azure sky, and the feel of the warm sun's rays upon my face and hands and penetrating my clothes.

That morning's journey along Laggan's side was a memorable one for the promise of the clear still dawn was maintained. There was something about the purity of the sunlight, a glazed effect over mountain, moor, and water, which belongs perhaps only to this part of Britain on a fine day in late autumn. In a wayside crofter's garden flowers still bloomed gaily—foxglove, Michaelmas daisies, roses, a little nest of summer, there by the loch side.

For some way an old cormorant, the first life I had seen on Laggan, kept pace with us just above the waves. He was logging thirty-five miles an hour by our clock. The surface of the road from Newtonmore to Spean Bridge was the worst we had met so far, with the exception of those around Inverness, and far more bumpy than any we had found in far-off Sutherland. We had to travel about ten miles an hour to avoid what, in caravanners' parlance, is known as 'shunting' which speaks for itself.

We had some post to collect in Fort William and, not wishing to take the caravan into the rather narrow streets of that pleasant little township, we left Romeo close to a garage a mile distant, going on in the Landrover to get our shopping done. By the time we had finished it was near midday. We coupled up, after twiddling Romeo round so that he faced north again, and rumbled onwards up the Great Glen, past Loch Lochy, to the turn for Glen Garry and Strome Ferry.

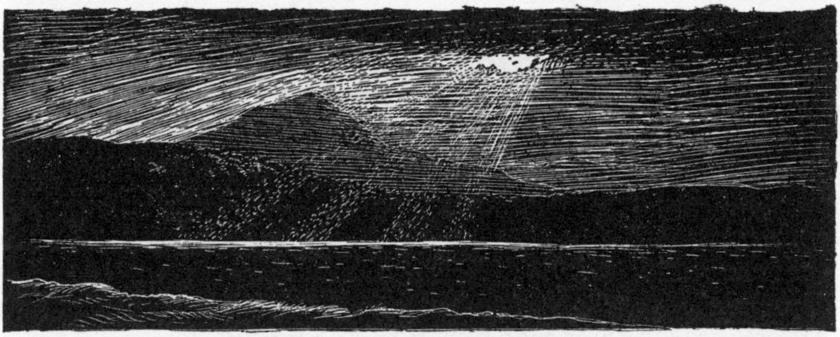

CHAPTER THIRTEEN

Hallowe'en in far Glen Garry

On Hallowe'en I took my stick and binoculars and climbed away among the bracken, following a winding sheep track. The light was going fast. Below me through the dark oaks the waters of Garry gleamed wanly, echoing the light of a wild, pale sunset sky in the west. The bracken smelled divinely, a sort of herby peaty smell. Now and then I pushed through bog myrtle whose delightful scent is such a stranger to the Midland plain. Very soon I had left the caravan behind and was in as wild a wood as one could wish for. It stretched away upwards, giving glimpses between silver-stemmed birches of corridors of tawny red rush and bracken, their furthest corners cloaked in dusk; more birch and yet more bracken, and many a knoll, and flat, and dell, threaded with silver black-banded stems.

There were no blueberry bushes here as in Glen Affric, and the woods seemed quite devoid of life. I was reminded of those unending forests of Labrador where, I have read, one may walk for many days and see no living thing. Very soon I was lost in a maze of brackeny dells and hummocks with the light growing ever more dim. By one knoll there was a hollow full of brilliant green moss; it was, I suppose, about twice the size of a washing bowl. I found it to be a miniature bog, quite a deep one, for my walking-stick thrust down never found bottom.

The sheep track I was following twisted here and there, as clear-cut as a gamekeeper's woodland path. When it came to a barrier of fallen birch (and there were many in this glen) it wound about, always tending up hill. I suppose the heavy-fleeced, black-faced sheep come down from the high tops to the cosy glens at the onset of winter. I had expected to see no living wild creature save sheep, but I was soon to find I was mistaken.

At one point (when I was passing a brake of fallen birch and tall red bracken, whose tiers of branching fronds rose one above the other in serrated layers) there was a sudden rustle. There regarding me, twenty yards distant and no more, was a red deer hind. Her great dark eyes were wide with suspicion and fear, her ears spread. Then she leapt gracefully away down the dell, crossing an open spot in front of me. She was followed by two much smaller beasts. All their coats were rough and dark, matching very well the russet tones of the bracken. What sanctuary they must find in Glen Garry! For I would call parts of it, at any rate, a cosy winter-defying glen, with plenty of warm bedding and fodder for the wild things of the hills.

By the time I regained the road which led me back to camp the light had nearly gone. Wild and fine it was; looking back up the glen to the head of Garry, with the last gleams of day reflected in the heaving waves, for a shrewd wind bustled the waters of the loch.

How cosy it was to see the shining orange light in the window of the caravan, down over the brae among the branching fern and guardian oaks! What a sight for an autumn evening and a returning traveller! Perhaps it was the trees I had missed most in far away Durness. Give me the wooded glens where wind and winter can be kept at bay!

Goodnight to the Isles

As I walked that night among the gathering shadows up Glen Garry I thought how easy it would be for a hunted man to hide there. If he had a gun and a rod he would come to no harm. There is many a cosy shelter he could find in those wild hills.

* * *

After supper, a very good one of mutton chops, cabbage and potato, followed by cheese and biscuits, and coffee, I lit a 'yog' (gypsy term for fire) close by the van. I gathered together birch twigs and oak logs and soon had a scented fire glowing. By the light of it I played my pipe, mournful tunes of my own composition and various renderings of Highland airs which I considered were in accord with my surroundings. The fire was greatly assisted by an old nightdress of Cecily's which was brought out for cremation. By then the wind had died, and it was a fine still night with the moon shining on the calm loch below us.

We sat side by side on a log by the fire playing our mournful tunes which sounded well in that wild place. The scent of the wood smoke and the gleaming flames reflected on the oak trees overhead were greatly to my taste, for what is life in the open air without the scent of wood smoke, and a dancing flame to sit by?

As every Scotsman knows it is on this night of all the year that 'ghoulies and ghosties' are abroad.

As we sat there with the fire-light on our faces, ruddy and warm, watching the little sparks fly upwards among the birch leaves, Ping's ears pricked and she gave a low growl. A man was going by on the highroad. He had a pack on his back and a stick in his hand, and his face was set up the glen. He looked neither to the right nor left. Where was he going at this late hour and in this wild place? Lone travellers at night always intrigue me.

At an early period of my life I was forced by circumstances to live in London, shut away from the grass, and the trees, and the scents and sounds of the sweet winds. Often at a late hour when I heard the double beat of feet passing along the pavement under the pools of gaslight, I would lie and wonder how life was using that unknown man or woman. Faint at first, growing near, then dying away into the distance. As a child I was fearful of the sound of footsteps heard from a long way off and gradually coming close. It was, I think, a sort of primitive fear, which I experience even now.

We heard the steady beat of this stranger's feet a long while after he had passed; the sound increased our sense of loneliness and our satisfaction, too, for the fire was warm, and our home was close at hand among the bracken.

I recounted all the most creepy ghost stories I had ever heard and we decided that footsteps in the night are perhaps the most hair-raising tales of all. There is something fearful in the thought of the restless dead.

A man I knew, who was a great climber and who delighted in exploring the less-frequented parts of Sutherland and Caithness, was one autumn afternoon overtaken by storm and darkness whilst in the vicinity of Sandwood Bay, scene of the mermaid episode described in an earlier chapter. He was forced to take shelter in a ruined crofter's house and all night long he was disturbed by ghostly footsteps and what was more horrible, perhaps, the sound of deep and heavy breathing.

This ruined house must have been Sandwood Cottage which has the reputation of being badly haunted and which is well known in the district. Other people have had uncanny experiences there, including S. D. Bolton, author of *Scotland's Western Seaboard*. He too was forced to shelter there from a storm whilst exploring the bay. He says in his book: 'When inhabited, this must have been the loneliest cottage on the mainland of Scotland. Now that it was deserted and ruined it seemed the most desolate spot on earth. But once inside I had the eerie sensation of being watched. I felt as a strange insect might feel on the slide of a microscope. I could find nothing among the wreckage of the interior to offer a clue to this unusual feeling. It is possible that imagination plays strange tricks when one is tired to the point of exhaustion, but I must admit to preferring the known horrors of the inferno outside to the unseen mysteries of the interior.'

Alexander Gunn, the same old man who had seen the mermaid, knew Sandwood Cottage well, for he once spent a night there when he was shepherding in the neighbourhood. He slept in an upstairs room and all night long he heard footfalls moving from room to room below. He had an explanation for the haunting. It concerned an Australian who came on several occasions to stay in the cottage for the fishing and later died in his native land, saying he would return.

It would be a brave man who would spend a night there alone—I would not do so for all the money in the world!

* * *

It would have been better if our midnight traveller in Glengarry had sung, as Robert Louis Stevenson's traveller had sung, 'lit internally with wine' as he went by his fir wood in the Lozère.

'Play me a Highland lament,' said Cecily, putting another log on the fire. But I could think of nothing but the hymn *To Be a Pilgrim*. Anyway, it was the only tune I could coax from my tin pipe which was recognizable.

Then from the north we heard a music far superior to mine. At first it was on the edge of hearing but growing all the time. It was the double musical note of wild whooper swans.

What better time or in what more suitable place could we have had this experience? The birds were, of course, invisible, and they were passing westwards for the sea, probably for the Kyle of Lochalsh where their fellows gather each winter. No doubt these were migrants, they might easily have just arrived from some far tundra, from some 'steel grey lagoon that no man knows'. Those musical notes, which have more poetry in them than even the cry of the wild pinkfooted geese we had heard at Braco, were signal cries, telling each member to keep station as they drove on through the dark.

No man quite knows how wild birds steer their way, it may well be some sort of radar. We know that fog confuses them and that then they are utterly lost, which to the layman, suggests they navigate by well-known landmarks. That could well have been so on that Hallowe'en in Garry. The stars were shining; below the birds would lie the familiar pattern of pale loch and river, a pattern handed down from one generation to another back into the mists of time. No doubt they saw the pin-point spark of our fire, and wonder stirred in their delicate craniums.

James Fisher and R. M. Lockley in their book *Sea Birds* have this to say: 'Sun or astronomical navigation seems to be the most satisfactory explanation so far; and more research into night migration might reveal that the migrant is guided by moon, stars, pre-glow and after-glow, which may assist it to keep on a course already begun before the sun or its glow has left the sky.'

* * *

At last the music, like the footsteps, sank to silence; there was nothing but the snicks and rustles of our dying fire. It was time for bed.

CHAPTER FOURTEEN

Garry Salmon Hatchery

THERE had been snow during the night, the high tops were white when I pulled aside the curtain and looked out. Perhaps the wild swans had been coming in before the storm as woodcock do in the south.

Out on the loch, a strange swell, like the wash of a steamer, was rolling along the surface. There appeared to be no cause for this, no wind was stirring the leaves in the glen. Perhaps it was a 'water horse' or monster on the move.

I had seen few trout rising since we came (which was no doubt due to the colder weather) and I sighed to think the season had ended and my little spinner, which proved so deadly, could not be tried out here. I could at least visit the salmon hatchery at the head of the loch.

This was built about five years ago, so the attendant told me, and is an entirely non-profit making concern run by the North of

Hinds in the glen

Scotland Hydroelectricity Board. The ova are obtained from a salmon trap in Loch Garry, and are taken from the female fish in November. I was surprised to learn that the eggs take five months to hatch. There are seven large circular ponds, each holding approximately 6,000 fry, in water about three feet deep, covered with netting to keep off the herons which will even come close to the road and buildings to catch the fry. The attendant fed the fry for us with liver, which he threw into them with a spoon. The water 'boiled' as the fish jumped for the food. Compared to coarse fish the salmon is slow-growing. We saw yearlings which were no more than three to four inches long. Once they are released and go down to the sea they grow quickly. When they are netted they are marked in the dorsal fin by a clip. It has been said they stay in the river near the point of release for another two years before going to sea, and they will not return of course until they are mature. They live to be about ten years old, so I was told; I should have thought they lived much longer, for coarse fish, such as carp, live to over thirty, and possibly longer. Two-year-old fish, which we saw, were silver and spotted, with the bars which are so characteristic of salmon parr.

The fry from Garry were not for sale. All the fish are marked and placed in rivers so that we may learn more about the still mysterious salmon, which, because it spends much of its time in the deep sea, defies continued scrutiny. I have in the past criticized the North Highland Electricity Board for altering many of the glens, and it was nice to learn that they are making compensation, in some measure, with this salmon fishery on Garry. At the same time, the general opinion of well-known anglers is that the Hydro-electricity Board have not improved the fishing on the Garry—far from it. An interesting article on this very subject appeared in *The Field* for 25 September 1958, in which the author was considering the sport to be had there before the fishery dam was built and after. In his opinion there is a marked difference. Apparently the volume of water going into the river is controlled from a trickle to a full spate, and the salmon dislike running up the powerful thrust of the turbine.

* * *

As we came back from the fishery we saw two buzzards sitting side by side on top of the telegraph post along the loch-side road; they looked as big as eagles. It is curious how they like perching on telegraph poles; I have noticed it in other parts of the country, such as Wales and Devon. Seen close at hand, they are impressive birds with a proud bearing, and their colours are rich, like patterned autumn leaves. I have only once seen a nest with eggs. It was on an inaccessible ledge in Cornwall, in the sea cliffs. I was above the nest and could look down into it and see the five round blotched eggs. The nest itself is a bulky affair of sticks lined with wool.

When I went down to the shore to take a coloured picture I heard the croaking of ravens. Two came flying over at an immense height. They were some two hundred yards apart but were conversing as they flew, one with the other. They passed eastwards, still holding height, for Binneun forest and its bens, whose tops were hidden in cloud. For some time after they had dwindled from sight I still heard their guttural remarks. It puzzled me why they did not fly together as I imagined they were 'bird and wife'. When seen in flight they appear long in the neck and head, and short of tail. The wings, too, have a particular shape. I could tell a raven by its silhouette anywhere. The tail is not wedge-shaped, like the hoodie or carrion, but like the blade of a putty knife; and the heavy bill, which is a serviceable weapon, is much stouter and stronger than in others of the crow family. It is extending its range (so is the buzzard), but it can still be considered a scarce species. No other of the crows has that guttural croak which carries as far as the call of a wild goose and is always associated in my mind with the barren precipices and sea cliffs. Though now the raven is more or less confined to wild rugged country it was once common enough in central wooded areas of England, and up to the middle of the nineteenth century still bred in trees, usually ancient oaks, in some of the old parklands and forests such as Sherwood and Savernake, and even in Warwickshire.

That evening at dusk I heard a robin singing his sad little melody from a golden birch just up the brae. The last of all our wild birds to sing, and the only one who sings so late in the day, this was truly his evening vespers.

I thought of that little bird with the long dark months of winter before him, when food would be hard to win, and with solitary birds of prey ready to slay him for a meal. Yet the future did not concern him; this was the moment, in the evening hour, when after his simple day's work, a grub here and there, a worm, perhaps, by the burn-side mosses, he felt content, content with himself and this damp, dusky glen where no doubt he had been born. And I prayed that he would live to see and feel the coming of the spring, when the birches, now losing their last leaves, would be a new and tender green once more, and the bluebells would open their first lilac flowers in the hanging woods. Robins, unlike some other birds, are satisfied with their own company and are entirely self-reliant. Perhaps he sang because it pleased him to see us there, with the lighted van, and the signs of human activity gave him pleasure; or maybe that song was just to let us know that we were camping on his preserves. It is known that each has his own jealously-guarded territories upon which no other robin may encroach and this was perhaps a form of gentle remonstrance —we were there only on sufferance.

Next morning the loch lay becalmed, the surface so finely polished that one could almost see a piece of fluff floating far out in the middle. Here and there a tiny ring rose and widened as a troutling or dancing fly touched the surface. Every bracken frond and birch leaf held a trembling pearl of moisture.

We must have been placed at the correct angle to these hanging drops, with the sun in front of us to the south, for a bush of scarlet hips which grew among the bracken appeared to be clustered with precious gems. Some shone vivid yellow, others orange and blue, yet others violet, and one particularly fine rain drop was the colour of a brilliant glowing ruby. Nor were these brilliant sunbeams lacking in warmth. We opened wide the windows and felt the comforting rays flow in. Ping, ever a sun-worshipper, was quick to seize her chance. She leapt upon the back of the seat cushions, her favourite couch.

There is a fellowship between owners of pekes; they are a privileged race, for I know no dog which is more amusing, courageous, or intelligent. There was a time when I considered them lap-dogs, but anyone who is owned by a peke soon alters this opinion. Several things one soon learns about them. Their cushion is sacred; once ensconced upon it, they may not be disturbed. They prefer to sleep as humans do, with their small round heads pillowed at an angle and a blanket drawn up round their shoulders. They fear nothing—size makes no matter. They

have minds of their own. They will obey an order, but in their own time. No dog will give a warmer or more affectionate welcome when they have been separated from those they love; you get as big a welcome if you have been away an hour as when you have been absent for a week. No dog takes more care of its personal hygiene—they are as particular as cats. Pekes never cringe or fawn on you. They have the few good qualities the cat possesses without the drawbacks of that lesser animal. A peke, fed correctly, has its own little personal smell which is never 'doggy'. The trouble is that once you have owned a peke (or it has owned you) you will always have one for the rest of your life!

Ping is the only dog we have ever had who enjoys the TV. She has her favourite programmes and Semprini is her most admired pianist. She watches him and listens with rapt attention. 'Westerns' are popular and, of course, as might be expected, she finds Cruft's dog show of absorbing interest.

My other dogs, spaniels and retrievers, ignore the screen and never deign to glance at it. They are real television 'snobs'.

CHAPTER FIFTEEN

The Waterfall

ACROSS the road from our camp the bracken was almost twice the height of a well-grown man, while up among the woods in the sheltered hollows it was still green.

When I looked out of the window one morning, three little roe deer stood in a clearing hedged round with the delicate gold and red fronds. They were the first I had seen in Scotland. One, a trim little buck, lifted a back leg as I watched him, a leg as slender and graceful as that of a greyhound, and scratched his rump lazily with his little horn. They grazed for a while, showing their white 'flags' as they turned, these white hinder-ends which must serve so well as beacons to their calves. Then something scared them. They melted into the fronds which completely covered them.

When later that day I took my stick and glass, and climbed up the glen, I found their runs, like those of rabbits, which wound in and out of the branching bracken stems. It must be well past Christmas before these tall bracken forests are felled by the keen frost and the roe, and red deer too, must winter here on the steep hill sides.

It was a glorious frosty afternoon when I began my walk, but a mist lay over the loch and veiled the lower slopes of the mountains to the south. By following sheep paths and deer tracks I climbed away up the side of the glen, taking my time, and filling my lungs with the glorious air, the scent of which was beyond description.

Soon I heard a distant murmuring rush, yet perhaps it could be better described as some distant bulldozer at work. Surely they were not felling the trees? The sound seemed to get louder and then fade away, and for a long time I was puzzled as to what caused it. Soon I knew. It was the sound of falling water. I turned to my left and climbed up among the silver birches, whose trunks were a dazzling white in the sunlight, and the bracken, the colour of which was something no artist's brush and palette could ever capture.

In front of me the hill rose steeply with huge granite rocks protruding from the bracken, and over the top of a massive boulder I saw the fall at last. A tenuous veil of white water pouring over the top, to tumble into a deep brown pool at the foot.

Green ferns grew round it, the bracken arched it over, and, at one end, caught in an angle of a rock (a sort of miniature cliff) a raft of yellow birch leaves, like a tessellated table-top, gravely revolved. At the tail of the pool the water slipped away, a fulvous brown, shot with golden darts and coloured bubbles, to fall in another series of waterfalls down the steep slope towards the loch. The rush and roar of the water cascading down the smooth dome of rock filled the ears; underlying the main turbulence of sound were musical notes like kelpies piping on flutes of reeds.

To complete this perfect picture a scarlet-berried rowan leaned over and the bright fruit was reflected in the water. I looked back behind me to where the sun was westering, its lower half turning to a soft rose. Mist covered the loch, which lay, a lake of whiteness, of milk perhaps, from shore to shore.

I left the fall at last and climbed onwards to the crest where the bracken became shorter and the trees less. Then I was out on the open moor with its deep tones of madder, ochre, sienna, and buff. Few artists have painted the high tops at this time of year. Sir D. Y. Cameron's superb etchings and drawings give, I think, a truer picture of these hills than his paintings. The trouble is that the colours of the winter high tops are sometimes so rich and varied that they are almost gaudy, and people who have never seen them would never believe that they could be so full of brilliance.

Once out of the glen it was piercingly cold, even though there was no wind. I walked for some miles over the peat hags, passing several ugly-looking green bogs here and there, until I came to a low ridge strewn with boulders. I lay down among them and took out my glass. Ahead of me the ground climbed away to rugged peaks. In the middle distance was another waterfall whose voice I could just hear at intervals when a puff of lightest breeze brought me the sound. The white twisting rope of water fell from some considerable height down a mass of tumbled rock, and birch trees grew up the steep sides. Through the glasses it appeared to be a delightfully remote spot.

At first I saw no deer anywhere, though I searched all along the flanks of the mountains to right and left. I brought the glass back to the waterfall and systematically searched down the little glen below, where thickets of birch and uneven ground might hold deer. As I was looking through the lens I saw the horns of a stag emerge quite slowly from the little corrie—first the pale tips, then his handsome head and shoulders came into view. He walked across a little flat beside what was obviously a burn, and stood there looking towards me. He was soon followed by seven hinds of various sizes and colours (it is amazing how they vary in colouring). They grazed peaceably, all save one, the last to appear, who was constantly on the watch, turning her head first one way then another. It is the hind who is the sentry, the old stag leaves that duty to her.

It was fascinating to watch these lovely wild creatures in their natural home enjoying the afternoon sun. It was wonderful also to be able to project myself, through the magic of my powerful stalking glass, to within a hundred yards or so of them. I could even see some field-fares busy among the rowans by the fall, and a red grouse erect on top of a stone to the right of the deer. I felt almost ashamed to pry on their private lives, like a Peeping Tom.

The stag was not in restless mood, though once I saw him stretch his neck and his big mouth opened to emit a soundless steam (he was so far distant I could not hear his call). After

grazing in a desultory fashion he at last lay down in the sun under a heathery brae and swung his great head into his flank.

Not a bad life, I thought, short but vivid; better than many a human one, dragged out in some factory or slum, shut away from the air of heaven.

I closed the glass at last and began to walk across the moor towards the waterfall. As I did so the sun withdrew and a chilly mist came down. I thought nothing of this at the time, but walked on. The corrie with the deer in it was now hidden from me by dead ground. Three red grouse burst from the heather right in front of me 'back, backing' hysterically. They went curling away to my left and were lost in the veils of mist.

It is amazing how deceptive distances can be. Through the telescope the glen and waterfall had seemed so close, but it seemed to get no nearer as I walked on and the mist was thickening all the time. I came over the ridge at last and there was my objective, in front of me, and the sound of the fall was considerably louder than the one back in the glen. Soon I was walking among the birches where I had seen the deer but to my great disappointment they had gone; only some 'sign' was steaming gently on the short grass by the rippling burn. I thought of climbing this last ridge by the fall to see what lay beyond, but now the time factor had to be considered. I wanted to be back in camp in time for supper at least (tea was now out of the question).

When I glanced back across the moors the way I had come I was brought up short with a sense of uneasiness. A thick white mist had quietly shut down behind me like a sinister wall. Only the very top of the ridge in front of me was visible now, glowing a most rare mother-of-pearl as it caught the last of the sun.

I was annoyed at not being able to explore the little glen and more annoyed, perhaps, that the deer had gone for I had hoped to see them at close quarters. But there was nothing for it, I must get back to camp. So I turned around, and keeping the sound of the fall behind me, I set out over the moors.

Within, I should say, another five minutes, the mist had shut down, forming walls of white before and behind me. I could smell it, too, a musty peaty smell.

Now I pride myself on a good bump of locality. I have been lost before on the Solway marshes (which was a most unpleasant experience). Here at least there was no menacing tide creeping in to cut me off, filling the hidden gutters and brimming over as a full wine glass spills.

What was a little disturbing was the fact that the setting sun was now barely a guide; soon I did not know exactly where it was for the white wall wrapped me like a shroud. The only guide was the sound of the fall. I kept it behind me as well as I could, with its voice growing ever fainter, until I could hear it no more. I looked at my watch. It was ten past four, in another half an hour it would be dark and there was no early moonrise.

I walked on, I skirted soft ground—once I went in over my

knees, suddenly, and felt that curious warm dart of fear in one's vitals which one gets in an emergency. Of course I was in no danger, it was just stupid, natural reaction, I suppose. All the same, I did not fancy a night on the moor for it promised to be a hard frost. As is always the case at such times, my imagination began to paint the most exciting pictures. Cecily in the warm van, pretending not to be anxious, Ping on her cushion, the lamps lit, fog and darkness outside; the frequent going to the door to look and listen, only to see the white wall of vapour, in the gas-light. I thought of what she would do during the hours' slow passage from midnight on to dawn, the fear, the panic, and then (let's go the whole hog!) search parties from Invergarry—sturdy men, used to the hill mists and the corries, ghillies, and stalkers, shepherds, and perhaps even a rangy Laird or two! Then the police, with their chequered peaked caps, stretchers, tracking dogs, and finally to the last grim scene: the discovery of the inert body lying among the heather, with the dew-like hoar frost on the jacket, something which had to be lifted on to the stretcher, no longer a 'him', but an 'it'. Perhaps they wouldn't find me until the spring and the melting of the snow!

I walked on. The light was now diffused all over, not dark, not light. I seemed shut in a white room. Visibility must have been about two feet, possibly even less. I knew after walking through endless peat hags and heather, with here and there a rock, that I was well and truly lost. I literally hadn't the foggiest notion where I was!

* * *

I looked again at my watch. It was now ten minutes to five. I had been walking for forty minutes. All at once a splash! A loud grunt, rather like a boxer hit by a low blow! I jumped like a kangaroo.

A huge, misty shape dashed past my front—either a stag or a hind, I couldn't tell which, and I wasn't particularly interested in natural history at that moment! For some moments I heard its splashing bustle through the mosses, then silence.

On the road to Loch Hourn

I stood still, at my wits' end. Perhaps this wretched fog would clear, but there was no sign of it doing so. It might last all night, all tomorrow, even the next day! Anyway, keep walking, I told myself, keep walking and listening. Curiously enough, though it was now past five o'clock, the mist about me made the night quite luminous. But it was most uncomfortable walking, really most trying! I kept stubbing my toes on hidden boulders, and once I ran full tilt into a rock as big as a pantechnicon; and I wasn't too keen to go head first into a bog. I'd rather meet death on the tide-way than in a bog, which suffocates you at leisure, like a fat boa constrictor.

Now and again I would stop and listen, but there just wasn't a sound, not the call of a bird or the bleat of a sheep, nothing! Thick fog seems to make all things dumb. After I'd been going for another quarter of an hour I heard in the distance a whispering rumble. I stood and listened carefully because I wanted to make for that sound, it was the only movement in a white tomb. I began to edge towards it, cupping my ears. Once I thought it was to my right, the next moment, surely, it was on my left, then it was behind me. But after another five minutes I knew I was going to get there. This must be the waterfall I had seen earlier in the afternoon, at the top of the glen, when the sun shone on the birches and the red-golden bracken.

Louder came the sound through the fog. It struck me as rather an awful noise coming like that out of the wall of white. Louder still, *too loud*! It sounded uncommonly like the waterfall of the deer. IT WAS! I was back to where I started.

I sat down on a stone, not because I particularly wanted to, but because I sort of fell over one, backwards, and finished up with a bruised coccyx, which, to those who are shaky in their knowledge of anatomy, is our rudimentary tail. And I was aware that I was very, very thirsty, horribly hungry, and fairly steaming with my exertions.

I found a burnlet trickling through the mosses and threw myself headlong on the soft ground and drank the ice-cold stream. I felt in my pockets for a possible half-packet of chocolate which I had meant to take along and hadn't. I remembered now I had left it on the caravan table. Ping had probably eaten it by now, for she is a little pig for chocolate.

I began to wonder then whether I'd better stay where I was, light a fire, and get some shelter. There was fallen wood handy by the birch trees, enough to keep a fire going all night. If it hadn't been for Cecily I might have done just that, but I must confess too (and this without shame), that I sensed something uncanny in my surroundings. There flitted through my mind the story of the terrible Fear Liath Mor, the Big Grey Man, which haunts the summit of Ben Mac Dhiu and has been seen and heard by several level-headed, educated people such as the late Professor J. N. Collie, a former president of the Alpine Club.

It is easy to imagine ghostly apparitions and inexplicable sounds, especially in misty weather, in these wild high places, and no doubt my nerves were in a strained condition. But I was aware that from time to time, above the ceaseless tumbling of the fall, I clearly heard a curious sharp 'clack', as of one large rock being struck against another, or of a stone being hit repeatedly with a hammer. The sounds were not regular, sometimes there was a minute's or so pause before I heard it again. I must confess I soon abandoned all idea of staying the night there alone, even with the company of a fire.

I rested there, from sheer exhaustion, for about twenty minutes and then set out again. I knew that if only I could keep a straight line the glen wasn't more than a couple of hours walking to the south. Then I hit upon the idea which I should have done before, of following the stream. I knew it must find its way somehow down to the glen as long as it didn't go underground as they often do, and as long as it was the right glen (I just dared not think of the alternative).

I found the burn without much trouble. I couldn't miss it because the fall guided me to it, and I began following it. This wasn't all that easy because of the rocks and soft ground. Once I thought I was bogged for I went in up to my knees. After some hours' walking, just when I was beginning to feel all in, I heard a sound which cheered me a good deal, another waterfall! Then a birch tree loomed up in front of me, then two more, then the bracken. I was on the edge of the glen; the ground fell steeply below me. Here the fog had thinned considerably and I found my bearings. Even so, it was some time before I hit the hard road. I got stuck in seemingly impenetrable thickets of bracken higher than my head, and once I fell into a boggy hollow and went up to my arm-pits in black mire.

I can only say the road felt very good under my feet when I eventually reached it, and a faint radiance, shining through the gloom, which was the caravan window, was even better. Very soon I heard Ping giving tongue, and a sudden glow showed as Cecily flung open the door. It was ten minutes past two in the morning.

After all, I think Cecily had had the worst of it.

CHAPTER SIXTEEN

To the White Sands of Keppoch

We went into the Tomdoun hotel for a drink. I felt in need of one after my recent experience, and my back was still painful after my fall. Over the bar was a magnificent *salmo ferox* which, to the non-angler, is a loch trout.

I like stuffed fish (many 'can't abear' them), and if well done I find them particularly satisfying. When I was a small boy I caught a three-pound brook trout from a tiny Warwickshire stream, and after much subterfuge, managed to smuggle it to our local taxidermist. In those days to have a fish set up cost about three pounds, but somehow I scraped and saved to pay for it. It is above my desk as I write, an ever-present reminder of a far-off April morning, a damp meadow with cowslips, the first cuckoo's voice calling from the field elms, and a triumphant small boy.

This magnificent specimen in the Tomdoun hotel was caught by the proprietress, Mrs Grant, in September '57. The salmon fly which helped to achieve its downfall is mounted beside the fish. It is small-headed and of perfect proportions, and weighed seventeen and a half pounds. Its length was thirty-three and a half inches, and the experts say it was sixteen years old. It was caught in the smallish Loch Poulary, which one can see from the hotel windows, and perhaps one day I shall try and catch a bigger one there. These huge lake trout have always fascinated me. Macdonald Robertson, in his *In Scotland With A Fishing Rod*, has some interesting chapters on his experiences with these fish, which are mostly caught by trolling and not with the fly. He did, however, catch one of fifteen and a half pounds, on the fly, in Loch Awe, which holds some vast specimens of *salmo ferox*. Charles St John, who was as handy with the rod as with the gun, advises that if you would catch a really big *ferox* you should troll with a good-sized bait, 'not much less than a herring', and not to begin trolling until two o'clock in the afternoon. He seems to make a great point of this. He believed that Loch Ness, of all the Highland lochs, held the record *ferox*, but some very good specimens have come from Loch Ericht in Inverness-shire. The record *ferox* weighed thirty-nine pounds eight ounces and was caught by a Mr Muir in 1886, I believe in Loch Awe. St John avers that *salmo ferox* is far more destructive to trout fry than the most voracious pike.

As we went on past Loch Poulary that morning and saw it glittering in the sunlight, I longed to be able to have some radar eye which could pierce those depths and see which was the biggest *ferox* there. Somehow it seemed to me a most fishable water and not too large. An immense loch such as Ness or Shin (which, incidentally, holds some fine *ferox*, too) seems to dishearten an angler before he ever begins operations, for the chances of your ever being at the right place at the right time, quite apart from the mood of your quarry, means that the scales of chance are heavily weighed against you. I have trolled for *ferox* in Loch Awe without success, but I was fishing in the morning, and thus disregarding the advice of Charles St John.

* * *

The fish quays at Mallaig

We were on our way that morning to Loch Hourn, the deepest and blackest of all the Highland lochs, and it well lived up to its name, the Loch of the Evil One.

The road from Tomdoun to Hourn is narrow and with frightful hills. We could never have attempted it with the van in tow, and eventually, after climbing some spectacular gradients, and turning some more than hairpin bends, it petered out a little way along the south side of the loch with barely room to turn the Landrover. The water is as black as ebony and even close inshore is of immense depth.

A mighty storm, as menacing as the mouth of Hell itself, came working up over the mountains and we fled before it back to Garry, and saw rainbows spring out all around us.

* * *

What happens if one meets a fellow caravanner on that long and tortuous road which leads from Fort William to Mallaig? It is one of these problems to which I have not yet found an answer for, so far, the occasion has never arisen in my travels along 'one-car' width roads. Caught between passing places it must be a tricky business for there are few who can back successfully with a van in tow; the stern slews left and right, and you can't get off the road despite skilful manipulations of the wheel. We passed along the Mallaig road therefore with some anxiety, scanning the twisting ribbon ahead as keenly as mariners navigating in a fog. But always it lay empty save for ubiquitous hoodie crows and an occasional buzzard hunched morosely on a telegraph pole.

Before the second world war this road from Fort William to Mallaig was notorious for its bad surface which resembled the bed of a mountain stream. No pleadings of the Mallaig townsfolk could get any authority to act. It was the last war which changed all this and much of the surface is now respectable for three quarters of the way.

There is a story of sixty tourists who made the journey by car to Mallaig before the war, and they were so fearful of the return journey they put their cars on the rail rather than face the road.

* * *

Poor little Ping was in trouble. During our sojourn in Garry her right eye had turned a milky blue, and the poor little thing was obviously in pain. She sat listless and shivering, with her soft round head held on one side and both eyes closed, reminding me of a rabbit infected with myxomatosis. They only opened fully when she smelt food, or heard the rustle of chocolate paper. So *en route* from Garry we sought out a vet in Fort William, a Mr Carmichael, who lived up in the high 'toon'. He found a dead eyelash was the cause of the trouble and removed it skilfully. When we asked him how much we were in his debt, he would have none of it—one more example of the kindness and warm-hearted character of the Scots. On many occasions in our travels we met with little courtesies and kindnesses which, I am afraid, a visiting Scot would not have found south of the Border.

* * *

Imagine a promontory of smooth green grass cropped close and fine, and large granite rocks protruding from it sealed with golden lichen. Imagine little bays of pure white sand, so firm and fine that even the bare foot leaves no imprint; add to this the white smother of rollers around the seaward skerries, and the blue hills of Skye across the sea, and the equally impressive silhouettes of Eigg and Rum, the one like the prow of an old-fashioned man-of-war, the other an impressive mass of rock against which the great Atlantic rollers thump and rave. Add again to these mental pictures the thin, lost keening of snow-white gulls, the whistling of innumerable curlews, the scents and sounds of tide-flung sea-tangle, and perhaps you will have a picture of our resting place at Keppoch.

We rolled off the road across the firm green turf and came to rest on the very lip of the sea which washed and swilled among the weedy skerries not forty yards away, where the smooth black heads of seals bobbed up in an inquisitive manner. What a change this was from the lonely silent glens with their mists and bracken, and the tumbling burns!

When, on 5 November, the sun shone with vernal warmth, and the distant outline of the Coolins were a magical mother-of-pearl above the blue line of the sea, Cecily and I went down among the grey rocks to a little bay of snow-white sand and there undressed and swam out into a clear rock-bound lagoon. I have had many a colder bathe in summer than that we enjoyed at Keppoch on 5 November 1958. It was as though we had been transported on some magic carpet back into the days of summer. All the ingredients were there, the vivid blue sea, the warm sun, the sleepy call of the gulls, even flies sidling and settling on the immaculate walls of Romeo.

After our swim we felt as if we had experienced a Swedish *Sauna* bath; we were tingling from head to foot and fit for anything. As we had lunch with the caravan windows flung wide, white herring gulls came and begged for bread, hovering above us with the sun shining through their vanes. One particularly greedy gull was very bold, seizing nearly every scrap we threw, right under the beaks of more timid mendicants. And Cecily, whose sense of humour sometimes takes quaint twists and quirks, concealed an aperient pill within a flake of bread and tossed it forth. One gulp and it was gone, though the bird looked thoughtful before he dived for more. There was much to do and see at Keppoch of the White Sands. We haunted the fish quays at Mallaig and saw the boats unloading crans of lovely soles and plaice whose glistening flanks and pinkish tails still moved a little as they lay, piled one on another, in their wicker baskets. (Though, alas! we could buy no fresh fish from the fishmongers in the town, who only had tired kippers and still more weary cod steaks.)

We watched the bustling departure of the Skye steamer with its attendant cloud of gulls following the churning wake. We explored that lovely road which runs by Loch Morar where the unhappy old Lord Lovat sought refuge on one of the wooded islands after

Culloden. (The redcoats ferreted him out and he was beheaded on Tower Hill, where he met his fate, with great bravery, at the age of eighty.)

I do not suppose that there are finer sunsets anywhere than those to be seen from the mainland 'over the sea to Skye'. As I sat fishing for bass from the rocks (using the same spinner which had won us so noble a supper way back in Sutherland), I saw the greens and golds and banks of cloud beyond the soft silhouette of Rum and Eigg, and thought of that Victorian painting, by an artist whose name I cannot recall, which was entitled *Goodnight To Skye* . . . an upturned boat upon a lonely shore, with the last light gleaming on the waves; the sort of picture which would fill our modern long-haired charlatans (who pose as artists) with sneering scorn. Of course we observed Guy Fawkes' night with due solemnity. When it was dark we went down to the shore below the van with three rockets. These were stuck in a bottle neck and discharged in the direction of the Sound of Sleat. They made an impressive hissing arc over the dark sea and I hoped the Mallaig lifeboat would not be launched in consequence.

On our last evening I took my spinning rod and again tried for bass from the rocks. Over towards Skye the sky was primrose pale, barred with soft grey cloud, and Rum and Eigg were dark silhouettes against the dying day. Rum, especially, seems from the mainland, a grim inhospitable place. It was difficult to imagine that it is inhabited, but it is (very much so); for it was, and I believe still is, known as the Forbidden Island and nobody is even allowed to land there, which seems an extraordinary state of affairs.

In A. M. Dunnett's fascinating little book *Quest by Canoe* (which contains a momentous and breath-taking account of crossing the Shuna Sound, in his canoe, surf-riding the waves), he describes how he and a fellow canoeist defied the ban, landed, and made camp, to be immediately challenged by a keeper. The following conversation took place.

'Have you permission to land here?'

'Yes.'

'Who from?'

'Ourselves.'

Dunnett and his friend then proceeded to set up their tent, completely ignoring the unhappy keeper, who was probably just as uncomfortable about the whole business as they were, having been ordered to turn them off by the owner of the castle. In this instance things ended smoothly, but Dunnett gives the impression that this ban on visitors is regarded with great disfavour by the local Highlanders. He says that the adjacent township of Mallaig and villages on the islands and mainland have many stories to tell of indignation and reprisals, and that from time to time revenge is taken and the deer are raided. As he says, there is an unhappy atmosphere and no wonder. Things may be different now (Dunnett's book was published in 1950); I trust they are.* Let us hope the time is not far distant when the wild places, the mountains and islands, will be free of access to all men. Already the national parks are extending their territories, and I, for one, am glad.

There will never be much nuisance from trippers, the *wrong* kind of trippers, in the remote places, only the young, adventurous and fit will climb the high mountains, and it is utterly wrong that a few selfish rich people, in many cases Sassenachs, should have the effrontery to keep anyone off their land unless they are poaching game. It is a form of selfishness which does an enormous amount of harm.

But let me turn to pleasanter things, and to my rock overlooking the sunset sea at Keppoch.

The tide was going out, stirring the tassels of glistening seaweed, whilst up in the dark wet crannies of the rocks it thumped and gulped with loud reports and bursts of spray.

I felt a tug on the spinner and caught a saithe, just too small to keep. It lay momentarily on the rocks with despair in its round goggly eyes. I slipped it back into the stirring weed tangle at my feet, one glimpse of a darting shadow, and it was gone. It was late when I made my way back across the bay of the white sands, and in the shadows I met a crofter, and we talked until dark. In

* I understand Rum has now been taken over by the Nature Conservancy.

Commando memorial in the Great Glen

his youth he had been ghillie and gamekeeper; as a lad he went down to Sussex, to Petworth, where he stayed keepering for a while. But his heart lay in the northern glens, by this western sea, so he came back, keepering for a time at Aviemore.

He told me that twenty years ago Seton Gordon, the great Scots historian and naturalist, used to walk the hills near Aviemore and when he came upon the keeper's gin traps, he used to spring them. Good for Seton Gordon and the hill foxes, but irritating for the keepers! This crofter told me 'we were mad at the mon, but och, he's a grand piper!'

In a recent letter to me about the incident Seton Gordon says, 'I wonder whose traps I sprung! I once found a golden eagle hanging upside-down in an eagle trap. I had to amputate its foot. It was literally as light as a feather, and must have been hanging upside-down for days. It rose to a great height and its mate left her eyrie to join it in the air. I often wonder if she brought it food for a time until it became used to life with one foot.'

It must have taken considerable patience, skill, and even courage to liberate the poor bird, and let us hope that after its dreadful agony it survived and maybe is still roaming the hills.

The name of Seton Gordon seems to be known throughout the Highlands wherever I have been. I should have thought that a man who has lived such a useful life and has so well recorded the beauty and ancient history of his land should have been offered a knighthood. Surely he is as deserving as a cricketer, or a jockey, or some ambitious politician?

The crofter told me that sometimes the wild grey geese come to Keppoch and he had shot them on the shore where we were standing, but they were only casual visitors. We fell to talking of fishing. He had been a ghillie for much of his life, and he was of the opinion that the two best fishing lochs in Scotland were Stack and Eilt. We had camped by Stack and passed by Eilt on our way to Mallaig. For some years he had held the sea-trout record for Eilt, a fish of seventeen pounds, but his brother, also a ghillie, had a sea trout of thirty-one pounds there in 1958, which, if true,

Mallaig Harbour

constitutes a record, for the sea-trout official record stood (or stands), I believe, at twenty-two pounds eight ounces.

The summer day when Cecily and I bathed was a weather-breeder. Like most things in life, you can't have a nice thing without paying for it.

When I had been talking to the crofter in the fading light, he had told me that there had been a gale warning that morning, but he didn't believe it. It seemed to me, as we talked there facing the pale west, where Rum was stark and clear against the last of day, that foul weather was surely brewing. Angry grey clouds, rolled like cotton wool, lined the rim of the sea, and there was a stir of wind about the rocks I didn't relish, yet it was quiet enough when we went to bed. We dropped asleep. This was about nine o'clock (we always went to bed early for the life of fresh air made us sleepy).

At about one o'clock Cecily and I awoke simultaneously. A full gale was blowing, the van shuddering under the impact. The wild weather at Durness and Staçk was thistle-down compared with this. We got up and turned out the oil stove, for at times we thought Romeo would go over. Then the gale switched a little. It began to back due west. The wind was now able to buffet us more viciously for Winston had been guarding us on our starboard side. There was nothing for it but to get up, dress, and move Winston up a yard or two. I pulled on my shirt, coat, socks, and trousers over my pyjamas, and tying my deerstalker flaps under my chin, went out into the bellowing darkness. Winston started, as usual, first push of the button, and I pulled him up eight feet on a level with Romeo's front. Then I fetched the winder and checked over the van legs. I found three could go down two inches at least, which accounted in a great measure for our rocking and bumping. My visions of our whole outfit taking wing over the rocks into the thundering waves hard by were now allayed. I returned to the van. The result of this manoeuvre was at once apparent; the van was steadier, we could feel the benefit of sturdy old Winston guarding us—he was indeed well-named. Out of sheer exhaustion, for we had been awake during the turmoil (and Ping had crept to us for succour, shivering with fright, in our bed), we dropped asleep, I to dream haunted sad dreams of loved ones lost. With one final vicious blow, which awoke us once again, just before dawn, the gale blew out like a candle flame. By nine o'clock when we awoke, it had whistled itself away over the Atlantic. A blue sea once again crinkled among the rocks, Skye was lit with sun from end to end, arched by one stupendous rainbow, and the snow-white gulls were in attendance on the rocks, head to wind, switching their bodies jerkily, like weathercocks, to each puff of breeze.

I have heard it said that the western Highland coast is the country of rainbows. This is true. Every day one would spring out somewhere, either over the sea or mountains; sometimes only a scrap was visible, an amputated rainbow, giving a queer stripe of colour in an unexpected place. I took many coloured pictures of these. What a wonderful invention is the camera, enabling one to capture these transitory moments of magical beauty, and enjoy them long after!

I was being prodigal with my films. I had tried to limit myself to say, 'I will buy no more', yet I would suddenly see some exquisite effect of light and shade and another film would be finished. I had set out with a pious hope that six Kodachrome films would see me through the trip; by 6 November I had got through three times that number. At twelve shillings a film, my finances were beginning to feel the strain. Some days we had to economize on food, yet we lived well, simply, and not out of tins like so many caravanners.

The crofter had told me that before long a wide metalled road will be made from Fort William to Mallaig. That means the hateful charabancs which are now shy of attempting the existing narrow rough track. When this is completed much of the summer peace and beauty of the white sands of Morar and Keppoch will be marred for ever.

CHAPTER SEVENTEEN

South to Fyne

INVERARAY, brilliantly lit by the morning sun, shone white, while the smoke from its 'lums' formed a level layer above it as we sat at breakfast on the south shores of Loch Fyne. Visible, too, were the turrets and towers of the Castle, and over my eggs and bacon I thought of the amusing story of Dr Johnson, when he was staying there during his 'Highland Tour' with Boswell. The Duke asked him one night, after dinner, to fetch from another room some *objet d'art* which he wished to show to his guests. Johnson did so, but with ill grace. To show his independence he whistled as he obeyed his host, much to the amusement of the Duke and his fellow diners.

Some woodcutter's fire up among the thick trees of the Inveraray policies was sending up a tall blue spire of smoke which, like the reek from the town, spread outwards near its apex like the cloud from an atomic explosion.

The night had been the coldest of the trip. Van and Landrover wore a fur jacket of rime, and the windows were patterned with designs so beautiful that a jeweller would have done well to note their intricate loveliness. The tide was at the flood, smooth as glass, and the hills of Argyll were sprinkled with snow, gleaming pink in the early light. Three otters were playing in the water not a hundred yards distant, dabchicks and cormorants were diving further out.

Since Keppoch we had travelled many miles and made pleasant camps in the wooded country close to Loch Creran. The only things of interest to me there were red squirrels and many bramblings, busy hunting for beach mast; some fat and sleepy seals sunning on a rock on the sea loch, and a pair of goldfinches which were twittering their liquid notes from the tip of a larch. These interested me particularly because they are by no means common in Scotland. Perhaps here I may digress a moment. As most naturalists know, this species became very scarce at one time in England, due to the attentions of bird-catchers for they were not difficult birds to net. Added to this, there is a high mortality among the nestlings (I will explain the reason for this in a moment), and during the early part of this century we were in danger of losing the gayest and most sprightly of all our finches. Then the law was passed forbidding trapping, netting and taking the eggs and young of this bird; this fortunately coincided with a depression in agriculture, and the consequent growth of thistles, the seed of which is the goldfinch's favourite food. All these factors helped to reinstate it and now, in many parts of the Midlands and the South, it is fairly numerous, especially in orchard country.

During the summer of 1958 I had under observation a pair of these charming little creatures which nested in the very tip of an apple tree in my kitchen garden. This is a favourite site, if the trees have been pruned (they do not care so much for the neglected orchards where no pruning is carried out), for the new growth bursting forth from the ends of the boughs affords a secret green arbour. They will always build right at the end of a bough. Elms and chestnuts are also thus favoured, and the nest is usually very difficult to see, for it is small, compact, and most beautifully made of moss and lichens and lined with feathers.

They delight also in young plane trees or sycamores, and you may often find a colony in our part of the country (Northamptonshire) in small trees bordering country roads. I have counted as many as eight nests in a quarter of a mile.

My pair at home spent about a week nest-building and this was the only time they betrayed the site. As soon as the hen began to sit, both parents became most secretive. The cock would never go to feed the hen if anyone was about. He spent much of his time singing on the top of a neighbouring apple, a delightful song, bright and rippling, reminding one of the play of sunlight on wind-blown leaves. It was a mystery to me when the young were fed. Only on very rare occasions did I see either parent visit the nest. Compared to the two and three minute visits of the tits and warblers when feeding their young, I doubt if these baby goldfinches were fed more than once in every four hours, and this is a point I have never seen noted in any bird book.

After ten days had passed the parents seemed to have lost all interest in the nest in the apple tree. To my surprise, they began to build a second one in a pear tree, some thirty yards away, again hiding the nest at the very tip of a bough.

I became mystified as to what had happened to the fledglings and imagined that a jackdaw had found them and eaten the brood. Jackdaws are the greatest enemy of the goldfinch, with jays a good second, and as my house is flanked by an oak wood where jays and jackdaws abound, I fully expected they had met with the usual fate.

One afternoon, unable to bear the suspense any longer, I procured a ladder and climbed up. The nest, I saw, was still there unharmed (usually when a jackdaw or jay has found it the nest is torn to pieces) but there was no sign of life as I put my fingers gently over the rim. To my dismay and astonishment, the whole brood, fully fledged, which had been cowering right down in the cup of the nest, burst forth like fragments of a bomb. Two could fly tolerably well and made a somewhat erratic flight to a tall box

November sunset on Loch Fyne

hedge hard by; the others dropped to the ground and darted like mice into the roots of the same box hedge. When I descended the ladder I could see no trace of them. I only managed to see one of the fledglings later and this was perched on the bough of a plum, keeping absolutely still like a little carved figure of a bird, and toning amazingly well with its surroundings.

I kept this mite under observation for the whole of that day and only saw the male bird come and feed it once though they were still busy finishing the nest in the pear tree. The next day the tiny mite had vanished. It never moved from its perch in the plum all the time I watched it. I saw it again three days later, a strong flyer, and it was being fed by both parents, who had not yet completed their second nest.

This second brood I left severely alone and had the satisfaction of seeing the whole brood flying with their parents, so they managed to survive.

Both the young of the greenfinch and the goldfinch must be a burden to their parents in their constant clamouring for food. As soon as they have left the nest and can fly strongly, they pursue their parents like a swarm of bees, giving them no peace, and keeping up a continuous twittering which, after a time, becomes quite unbearable to the human ear.

* * *

But to return to our journey. There were depressing signs that we were nearing civilization. Gone was the sense of solitude; traffic and people were back with us. In the woods of Bullividan, where we had a tricky site on soft ground under the beeches above the road, a shooting party awoke the echoes all about us one day, and keepers, dogs, and tweed-clad sportsmen eyed us askance, as we eyed them.

We had hoped to rest by Loch Awe and had travelled its whole length on the southern shore without finding a single place to make a suitable pitch, for there were no smooth verges and no old road on to which we could roll with safety. Even our pitch on

Fyne, delightful as it was, on a loop of disused road, was too close to houses for my liking. The southern bank is strewn with nasty little villas, built all along the old road, and traffic was passing continually. But the weather was making up for other deficiencies; it was frosty, clear, and sunny, and there was much to watch on this noble inlet of the sea.

Not far off shore I identified with the telescope a harlequin duck which was swimming near some eiders. This bird is described in Witherby's Handbook as a 'very rare migrant' but it has been seen before off the western coast of Scotland, notably in the Shetlands and the Outer Hebrides. Its richly coloured plumage was distinctive. So many collectors now breed ornamental ducks it is difficult to say whether the bird was truly a visitor or an escapee.

During January 1959 I watched for several days a snow-goose flying and feeding with greylags on the fields near the sea. The local Laird had told me that he knew of a man who lived across the Firth who had lost some snow-geese from his collection. This bird may have been one of them, but there was just no way of proving it. Many times I stalked within gunshot and even took a moving picture of it with a cine-camera. It was quite remarkable how when the skeins were in flight the snow-white goose shone out from its companions; you could pick it out with the naked eye from a distance of several miles, and on the ground it was even more conspicuous.

* * *

As we were having breakfast I was somewhat startled to see the conning tower of a submarine appear as quietly as an otter just opposite to us, out in the middle of the loch. She was HMS 527 and she surfaced and lay there like a basking fish. Soon the top of the conning tower opened and the submariners emerged, clad in white jerseys; they, like us, seemed to be admiring the beautiful morning and the view of Inveraray with its canopy of smoke. But they did not linger. Within a few minutes the figures went below and quietly and smoothly she sank from sight, leaving a glassy slick on the surface of the sea. It made us realize what potentially deadly killers are these ships of war, sly and silent assassins who are more at home under the water than upon it.

Seeing this submarine brought to my memory another picture from the 1914–8 war. I was a small boy walking with my father in the cliff woods by Babbacombe. Coming to a convenient seat we sat down to admire the view. Below us the winter sea was calm and grey, and white gulls passed to and fro. Without the slightest warning there appeared out in the bay, but close inshore, the conning tower of a German submarine, for we could clearly see the big U on its side. A man popped his head up with glasses to his eyes and for a moment or so quickly scanned the shore. Then the conning tower closed once more and in another minute she had gone. I often wondered if that particular submarine survived the war and was one of those surrendered at Scapa Flow.

* * *

Bonny the hedgehog seemed to have entered into his winter sleep. We did not like to disturb him but gently pushed aside the bracken and saw him curled up, with intucked black snout, his face invisible.

We spent an idle day going into Inveraray to renew supplies, which we did with some difficulty as most of the shops seemed to be closed for the winter. I had Winston replenished with anti-freeze as it looked as though we were in for colder weather.

The submarine re-appeared some way down the loch whilst we were on the quay, blowing clouds of steam from its side. When next we looked it had again disappeared. It seemed as playful as the two otters which came fishing up the edge of the dropping tide opposite our camp that evening. Their small black heads moved purposefully about, and now and then they dived, not with the kicking splash of a seal, but with the roll and furl of a big fish turning over. There seemed to be a great many of these attractive little creatures in Loch Fyne, for as we came back from

Inveraray we saw four or five diving and playing near the bridge by Cairndow. This loch seemed popular with 'submariners' for dabchicks, cormorants, and diving ducks were busy, as well as HMS 527.

That night a magnificent red sunset flared in the west. The best of this brief glory had gone by the time I got down on the shore with my camera, but I took one picture which proved a winner.

Next morning we climbed away up Glen Kinglas and Glencroe to the Rest and be Thankful, greatly altered since I saw it last in 1939. Gone were the tricky corners, the zigzag descent to Arrochar. Yet the old road was there, where we used to watch and gloat as the bull-nosed Morrises and other early cars panted and puffed, emitting clouds of steam as they climbed the long zigzag to the summit. We found a broad new road now with a firm mat surface and no sharp bends—truly the modern motorist is spoilt!

In Glen Croe the clouds were menacing, the glen full of gloom, fog rolled outwards from the corries. We later heard that police and shepherds were out on the hills hunting a sex maniac who had assaulted a little girl. Evidently he was making towards the Rest and be Thankful, but we never heard if he was caught. To catch a hunted man on such a morning, and in such a wild country, would be no easy task.

We came to the shores of Loch Long, suddenly and with surprise, and found the place little changed, though the hotel where Cecily and I had stayed had been burnt to the ground a few years back with loss of life. We had spent part of our honeymoon at Arrochar and I have recollections of rowing across the torpedo range, fearful lest the warning horn should go and one of the test torpedoes come tearing down the loch. One, I remember, went mad, leaping like a salmon from the water and describing circles, eventually hitting the rocks on the north shore with a reverberating clang. I remember, too, the fish we caught in the summer evenings, trolling down the loch with a spinner. We came back with baskets of mackerel and rock bass. The sea fishing was good, but over all hung the threat of war, and a week later

Chamberlain made his tired and broken speech, almost apologetically, it seemed at the time.

At the grocer's in Arrochar we purchased a nice fresh cabbage, the first we had seen for many days. The Scots, admirable race though they be (and I admire them more than Englishmen, perhaps, for many of their qualities) have a few small failings, one being the lack of interest in fresh green vegetables. Baps and bannocks are no food for the southern stomach. I often wonder that they, as a race, are so tough and brawny. Perhaps it is the 'parritches', or is it the haggis? They are not great fish-eaters, which strikes me as strange. One thing the Sassenach notices is the complete absence of beer as he understands it. Apparently it is not drawn from the wood, which is the way beer should be served, but from the tap. Invariably it has a great head of froth which necessitates much manipulation by the landlord. I was assured that this is looked for, nay, insisted on, by the customer, and beer without froth is regarded as flat. Also whisky should accompany beer, perhaps to add something to the flavour which is felt to be lacking.

As a connoisseur of beer this worries me. Bottled beer, of whatever brand, is distasteful to me—which reminds me of two pints of ale I shall never forget; one when I was a guest at the Athenaeum, the other in a Cambridge College. I have had other good glasses of beer in England but these stand out in the memory. A good beer should be mellow, full-bodied; you should taste the hops in it, it should have little or no froth upon its limpid surface, its flavour should not at once be apparent but steal upon one's senses at each pull at the tankard (for of course good ale should always be drunk from metal).

Coming over that melancholy and rather featureless pass of Glen Falloch, we could see the spidery electric pylons marching away over the great hills. What a stupendous job it must have been erecting them; some could only have been carried up on bulldozers. I had a most interesting talk with a man who was responsible for erecting these pylons in the Highlands. He told me work goes on all the year, winter and summer, for the stress of weather does damage to the cables on the high tops, and icing conditions are severe. The worst localities for erecting pylons are boggy lands where they have to sink firm foundations. He did quote me the cost of erection per mile and, if I remember aright, it worked out at about £3,000.

A few years ago, before the advent of the caterpillar tractor and bulldozer, such a job would have been impossible. These inventions have brought enormously increased power to tackling jobs of this nature, and are equally useful for destruction and construction. The ease with which a heavy bulldozer can push over a well-grown tree has to be seen to be believed.

Maybe the time will come when some better arrangement may be devised for carrying the power-lines. They do not improve the mountain scenery, although in some strange way they are impressive and seem to show a certain impudence and scorn of the highest and most forbidding terrain.

We turned left at Arrochar and followed the winding road beside Loch Lomond. The thick sturdy oaks were still in full leaf but the green tints were going and the road was strewn with acorns. Though Loch Lomond is perhaps the most famous of Scotland's lochs, both in song and history, though it is so close to the teeming thousands of a great industrial centre, it remains serenely beautiful, at least in the off-season when the charabancs and picnic parties have flown away. Dr Johnson came this way in the autumn of 1773 and it is interesting to learn that he visited an island in the loch which was 'planted with yew and stocked with deer', and another 'not more than half an acre, remarkable for the ruin of an old castle on which the osprey builds her annual nest'. It must be very many years since ospreys nested on Loch Lomond, and it is one of the very few birds mentioned in the Doctor's famous *Tour*.

We turned right before we reached Callander, and by the shores of Loch Vennacher we found our pitch, the only short strip of road which borders that handsome little loch.

It was a good site, a little peninsula grown with oaks, where there was a fine hard bottom and room to get both Winston and the van snugged down side by side under the leafy trees. The waters of the loch were glassy, freckled with rain drops. Scores of fat mallard were busy along the banks beyond our camp site. For a moment I wondered what they were after, and then realized they were gleaning the acorns which had fallen from the overhanging oaks. They kept well away from us. When Cecily went down to the little beach by our peninsula to get a can of water they all took quacking wing. The dismal evening meant nothing to us. The gas was connected, the lamps were lit, and whilst tea was being brewed I went into the bright tourist-battening town of Callander to get a newspaper and some fresh farm eggs, which I purchased just outside the town from a fine modern egg farm kept, I judged, by retired gentlefolk. These fresh eggs were welcome.

After tea we walked up the road in the gathering shadows. The oaks smelt damp, aromatic; numerous wood pigeons clattered off from among the acorns where they had gone to roost, and more mallard bustled away from under the overhanging oaks. To the right of the road the Forestry Commission had planted acres of larch, a favourite tree with me, and these were dressed in their full autumn yellow. But the colours on the other trees were going swiftly now, the birches were bare, and so were the beeches. Ash and lime showed their delicate architecture of twig and branch. Winter had almost come: everywhere dampness, the drip-drip of moisture, and a chill.

Beautiful as this country of Rob Roy may be, better known perhaps as the Trossachs, it was a different world to that which we had so regretfully left behind us. Even at that late season of November there were signs of the multitudes of picnickers and campers who had swarmed along the loch side in summer, leaving their filth, like hideous permanent droppings, on bank and shore. In the shallow waters of Vennacher, out from our little beach, empty tins gleamed, tossed there by litter louts. In this country we need the strict laws enforced by the Swiss. No paltry fine will stop this nuisance which becomes worse each year.

As a nation we are dirty and untidy, and must disgust visitors

Camp at Loch Vennacher

from Northern Europe. I can honestly say that at each of our camping places, when we left, no trace of our sojourn remained.

CHAPTER EIGHTEEN

The Old Red Hills of Galloway

As I got out of the Landrover on the shores of Loch Ken, stiff and weary after our journey from Vennacher, I heard the croak of greylags. I looked up and saw a couple flying overhead at a leisurely pace, down the loch. A greater treat was in store, however, for whilst Cecily was brewing up I heard the far-away cry of whitefronted geese, which surprised me. I looked up into the soft sky and for a time could not see them. Then they were there, at a tremendous height, coming from the north and heading west, no doubt for Luce Bay or the Sands of Cree. They appeared just as I have sometimes seen them in my dreams, faint misty chevrons and V-shapes, passing over in stately array. I was sure these birds must have just arrived from the Arctic regions where they were bred, for they were very high, and looked as small as swifts. Faintly their wild music died westwards and I went in to tea.

Just before dark I went down to the shore of Loch Ken to spin for pike. The record for Britain is reputed to have been caught there many years ago on a peacock's feather (why a peacock's feather I do not know). That historic fish, whose skull, I believe, was preserved for many years in Kenmuir Castle, weighed seventy-two pounds. The only result of my piscatorial efforts which were, I must admit, very half-hearted in the fading light, was to get my spinning line into another ugly tangle, which the patient and long-suffering Cecily again unravelled for me by the light of our lamps.

This had been a successful day's journey, and the last long run before we turned south for the Border. Only forty-odd miles lay between us and Galloway, where we planned to finish our wanderings. After the spectacular Highland lochs, Ken is like a reservoir in comparison. But there is a spacious beauty about it which attracted us. Many wild fowl, mostly mallard and tufted duck, were swimming out in the centre, though I saw no wild swans. Its shores were not built up with houses like the upper stretches of Fyne; it was still natural and wild, and had no sailing-club like that we had seen on Earn. Sailing-boats on a loch may look very nice and provide a great deal of fun for the lucky owners, but they suggest too forcibly a holiday-maker's playground.

Bonny, our little fellow-traveller, seemed to be well into his hibernation though the constant change of temperature must have puzzled him. When we had the 'blower' going in Winston, pumping hot air into the interior, the temperature was sometimes almost too warm. I had had this heater fitted specially for the trip, and we should have been miserable without it. The old type of Landrover was very draughty and uncomfortable in winter, but there was no draught in ours to worry us, even though it is a 'soft-top' model. These sturdy vehicles, which have a world-wide reputation as famous perhaps as that of Rolls Royce, are splendid starters in all kinds of weather. With Winston we never had a moment's trouble in starting, even after a damp, cold night, though like all cars he needed a warming-up period. No more suitable vehicle has been devised for caravan-towing for it will pull

Glen Garry camp fire

you out of soft places where an ordinary car would bog down hopelessly. This gives you great confidence. You can venture into places you would not otherwise attempt. The only drawback is the petrol consumption, about twenty-three to the gallon when towing fully loaded, but I doubt whether there is any other vehicle which is better in this respect.

As we went south that day we realized more and more how winter had arrived. The frosts had stripped most of the trees and what leaves remained were falling thickly in the still air. That night, just before we went to sleep, I gave a thought to our little promontory on Loch Vennacher with its ducks busy under the oaks. They would have the place to themselves now. No cosy lights would be shining through the darkness, only the deserted trees with the acorns plopping into the water, well over a hundred miles to the north of us. In such a tripper-scourged district we had indeed been lucky to find such a delightful haven for our last two nights in the Highlands. One other sign that we were well down the map was the absence of our old friends the hoodie crows. We saw plenty of crows that day as we came over the old red hills of Galloway, but they were all carrions, rascally vermin which have no redeeming feature whatever.

* * *

I was awakened on the morning of 14 November by the familiar cry of geese, the old whitefront music. I jumped over Cecily after extricating myself from my sleeping bag (no easy or rapid process), and opened the door. I was met by a dismal, foggy, raw morning with the far side of Loch Ken hidden in the mist. Right overhead was passing a great bow of whitefronts heading north. They were in a confused mass though the front, or bent edge of the bow held station. They were only just visible in the mist.

Evidently geese steer by Loch Ken. I was still puzzled as to why whitefronts should be so far up on the west coast of Britain. Three dabchicks, familiar friends now, were bobbing a few yards off shore among some tall slender reeds; one of them gave a clear rippling call.

Later as we were having breakfast, two greylags passed low up the loch, the same pair, I have no doubt, which went past the preceding evening, for they are creatures of habit. They were a little disturbed by the fog, I thought, for when they reached the head of the loch they wheeled, lowered their paddles, and came down on the water; soon drifting mist hid them from view.

By eleven o'clock we were on the road, pulling out of our Loch Ken site in drizzling rain. Somewhere in the village of Laurieston we took a wrong turning for Newton Stewart—my fault, as I wasn't following the map. Instead of taking the low road we climbed up over the desolate moors above Gatehouse of Fleet. Then the fog thickened and we had to run with sidelights on. Curiously enough, we saw more red grouse on this section of road than anywhere in our Highland wanderings. They sat in the heather on either side of the road, and one beautiful bird was perched on a stone wall.

When you see the red grouse hanging up in the poulterer's shop, or speeding away on sickle wings over the heather, you do not realize the wonderful rich, deep, purple-red tint of its plumage, which matches well the winter hues of the moors and peat hags. And that scarlet comb over the eye! How it adds just that extra spark of rich colour to make it a perfect study in harmony!

We dropped at last below the fog into the delightful hamlet of Gatehouse of Fleet. On the left of the road, I spotted a gem of a camp site among oaks, upon a promontory similar to that at Vennacher but more secluded and attractive. Below I glimpsed tidal waters and a stretch of sand and mud upon which hundreds of waders were busy.

This was certainly the most unusual site of our whole trip, this combination of woodland, rocks, sand and foreshore, and the estuary beyond which was thronged with waders. Curlews whistled as they flew out over the mud in droves, oyster-catchers piped, redshank shrilled; it was a bird-watcher's paradise. On a nearby tree was nailed a notice which read:

> 'Have you enjoyed your picnic? You have!
> Good show! Others will follow,
> So leave no litter.'

How much nicer this was than the usual 'Keep off, no camping', and threat of prosecution! There are some people, perhaps many of them with good reason, who will go out of their way to make things difficult for caravanners. I remember once, near Savernake Forest, being refused milk by a surly farmer. When we collected water from a nearby cottage from a most kind and obliging woman, the farmer got to hear of it and forbade her to let us have it. Her husband worked for him so he had the whip-hand. I thought that a particularly nasty spirit.

I was sad to learn from a brawny kilted Laird who later arrived (accompanied by two huge deer-hounds and a retriever), that during the summer picnickers left the place in a fearful mess with broken glass and filth everywhere. Yet for travellers like ourselves this kindly welcome warmed us through. We could lie in the van and hear the constant yodelling of the curlews, and when the tide was in the sea was only a matter of twenty yards distant from our little rocky knoll.

By the time we had finished tea the night had come, dark and misty, full of the wild sea scents of marsh and mudflats, mingled with the flavour of the thick-leaved oaks which formed a protecting grove about us. We were well off the main road and sheltered from any wind which might blow, whilst through our windows I could watch and study the teeming bird life on the flats. What more could I ask?

At three in the morning the flood tide came to the sandy beach and the pandemonium which broke out among the wildfowl was something I had never heard before, though for many years I have been wildfowling on the shores of most of the estuaries in Britain. Gulls, curlews, redshanks, and oyster-catchers were the chief vocalists; the yelping and the yodelling was continuous for over an hour. It awoke Cecily who lay grumbling and wakeful. I soon dropped off again for it was sweet music in my ears, though I missed the chiming of wild geese and whoopers. Occasionally, when a vehicle went by on the road to Stranraer, the sound was cut as if turned off by a tap, then a moment later it would start up again. This sudden cessation of sound which can be noticed not only in wildfowl but in other birds, such as starlings and crows, means that they have heard some sound which might spell danger. They will often stop their chatter even when there is no sudden loud noise to disturb them. They have learnt that enemies can creep up on them unawares under cover of a hubbub of voices; indeed, I myself have many times stalked a gaggle of geese while they have been cackling, and the noise of the dead reeds rustling, or the ice tinkling, has been drowned effectively.

This brings to my mind an amusing thought. We have all experienced the buzz of conversation at some cocktail party, or other social gathering when humans get together, and have heard the sudden quiet which falls. This has given rise to such sayings as 'an angel is passing overhead' or, in those countries beyond the Iron Curtain, 'the secret police are passing'. Few realize that this strange manifestation goes back a very long way, to prehistoric times, when the tribe had to be on the alert for enemies just as the wild geese have to be today.

I have never quite understood why wildfowl make such an outcry at the full tide. It may be dismay at not being able to get to their feeding grounds, the tidal flats, or it may just be anticipation of the feast to come. For after the tide recedes the dining-table is spread, freshly laid and replenished for the hungry guests. I think it may well be excitement at the coming feast. One other possibility is that they feel insecure. The vast vacant flats of sand and mud which offer them sanctuary are covered in water and none of the wader family likes to swim; they are happier on land, moist or otherwise. Only the ducks and divers delight in water for its own sake. That night was moonless and very dark (the warmest we had had), but that seems to matter little to the wildfowl of the tide. Their lives are governed by the moon, wind, and water.

Now and again, breaking in on the midnight concert, I could hear the deep 'augh augh' of the greater black-backed gulls. This fine handsome creature is as big as a small goose and its majestic wing-flaps are almost as leisurely as those of a heron.

Wild geese do visit this estuary of the Water of Fleet, as the river is called, but the young Laird told me they had not yet arrived. I was still mystified as to where the whitefronts were bound for that misty morning on Loch Ken. I longed for them to visit us in our little bay, but it was not to be.

* *

To be able to live for even a short space of time overlooking this fascinating bay was a delightful experience. Always its mood was changing, now hidden by drifting mist, now clear and sharp, with the winding tortuous channel shining with pearly lights, and the varied population of wading birds continually on the move. The mountain-bound Highland loch can never show the same lively stir, nor has it the sense of mystery which is always present on the smallest estuary of the sea. One must remember that a tidal estuary is also a busy airport for travellers. All the time passengers are coming and going, arriving from distant countries, and departing on the next tide. There may be a small resident population of curlews and redshanks, but the ducks and geese and many of the shore waders, such as whimbrel, godwits, and plovers, do not spend a great deal of time in one particular haunt. It is perhaps this sense of mystery which surrounds all gypsies that has so strong an appeal.

The beach just below us proved a treasure trove in the shape of innumerable shells of all shapes, sizes, and colours. A little burn ran across the sands not far distant and the head of this was a solid path of shells, all perfect and unbroken, washed clean and bright by the flowing stream of fresh water.

The hobby of conchology has always seemed to me a fascinating one. I believe there are certain localities round our coasts where a wonderful selection of shells may be found, some of them rare.

Robins were singing in the oaks around our van that evening, and the roof was thickly strewn with leaves. Across the road a pheasant went 'cocking' to roost; we might have been encamped in the middle of a wood. It was our last night at this site for on the morrow we expected to cross the Border. The chill fogs of late November were closing about us, and there was the long wet road to the South awaiting us, with the old humdrum life at the end of it.

CHAPTER NINETEEN

To Ullswater and Journey's End

OUR outfit was now showing signs of travel. Winston was masked with mud, mostly collected on our journey to the Mull of Galloway where the roads were miry. The van was no longer a gleaming grey but caked with dirt and dust, as though we had crossed the Sahara.

In Penrith, always, I think, a cheerful place with good shops and old-fashioned, comfortable inns, we turned right for Ullswater. Westwards the sun was a globe of rose, sinking into banks of fog. Ullswater, when we reached it soon after three o'clock, lay still and mist-wreathed, with the sinking sun making a path of molten brilliance across its mirror-like surface. It was not long before we saw our site for this, our last, camp, a delightful glade under an ancient spreading oak tree, right on the shore of this beautiful water; a tree which must have been seven or eight hundred years of age, with three great horizontal arms growing parallel with the

Washing day

ground below. We pulled off the road beneath it (the leaves were thick and hardly showed a trace of autumn), unhitched Winston, wound down the legs, and 'brewed up'.

As the sun dipped behind the fells, it grew a deeper rose and thousands of gulls passed over with leisurely wagging wings, most in formation like wild geese, and across the lake the towering fells stood out in flat blue silhouettes. There was a real sense of winter now, with the promise of frosty weather to come. Watching this procession of gulls (they were flying at different levels like bombing planes with attendant fighters), made me wonder if the name Ullswater was derived from gull's water, for I have seldom seen so vast an army as that which went past me that evening, high in the frosty air. They must, of course, have been bound for Morecambe Bay thirty miles distant, or they may, in winter, roost on Ullswater; but I saw none alight. All held their purposeful way to the west and the setting sun, and passed beyond my ken.

Sad to say, this our last camp was marred by a tragic discovery. Whilst I was away collecting wood for a fire, Cecily decided to tidy up the back of the Landrover. Whilst thus engaged she came upon Bonny's tin, from which, alas!, came the unmistakable odour of decay. On my return she confided her fears to me. When I investigated I found our little fellow-traveller had entered into the sleep which knows no waking; indeed, his demise must have occurred some days before, maybe during the bitter night by Fyne. Thinking back, I believe he may have been ailing when we found him in the sunny road by Bonar Bridge. It is most unnatural for night creatures, both birds and animals, to be abroad in daylight. I have found that barn owls hunting in full sunlight are often ailing birds. Rats seen abroad in daylight are usually near death. Maybe he had left the seeking of his hibernation place too long, and all our care had come too late to save him. Whatever the cause, he was dead, partly unrolled, infinitely pathetic, with his little black snout half-open, and his eyes closed. I took him to the hedgerow by the lakeside and there, in an ivied cavity, buried him with moss and leaves, one poor little Scots hedgehog in an alien land.

* * *

Supper over, I lit a fire by the hawser-like roots of the old oak which formed a natural seat. The bright flames leapt up, shining on the leaves overhead, and upon the huge horizontal branches, and it was good to sniff again the sweet wild scent of woodsmoke. A curlew whistled over the lake and above the fog, which lay like a white blanket over the water, and a sickle moon hung clear and sharp—sure signs of frost to come.

How lucky we had been with our camping sites! Here, after nightfall, nobody went by on the high road; we might have been the only people by the tarn. The only sound was the hooting of tawny owls, and the far musical bellow of a cow.

As I lay awake listening to the latter I was reminded that, to my knowledge, only one famous author has written in praise of the cow's voice, namely W. H. Hudson. He was a great admirer of the animal and has almost a whole chapter about it and its melodious bellow. Heard from a distance, this cow by Ullswater had a voice as precise and musical as the deeper notes of a bassoon. Perhaps it had been robbed of its calf, for no animal mourns with greater anguish if its child is taken from it.

To these pleasant, distant, homely sounds I fell at last into a deep peaceful sleep.

* * *

The next morning we were up at half past five for we wished to complete the run home in the day. It was clear, dry, and cold—so dry that with a handful of dead oak leaves (and purely out of sentiment) I started my last fire, which soon burnt merrily, whilst Cecily busied herself in the van. Overhead the morning stars still shone. The fells were clear-cut against the dim dawn sky, the tarn was without ripple. Somewhere a curlew was faintly crying, like the last echo of Scotland calling to us, the very voice of the wide hills, of the dear distant glens where, for a few brief weeks, we had made our camps, lit our fires, and led our wild free life.

I put a bough of dead oak leaves on the leaping flames. They flared up, making the tree above a floodlit fairyland of leaf, bough, and rugged bark. I thought of the little birch tree by Rannoch, alight, suddenly, like a torch in the glare of the evening sun; I thought of the wild gloaming by Stack, when I challenged the old grey stag; the tug of the fighting trout on my little spinning rod; the still majesty of moonlit Affric, with the path of silver light over the still water; and of my blind groping on the moor. One by one the memories came until, in the east, the sky was grey.

Cecily was putting the last touches to the packing of the van. In a moment or two it would be light enough to swing Romeo round preparatory to hitching on for the last leg home.

* * *

Half past three, 19 November 1958. Speedometer reading: 3,239 miles.

My hand went out to the switch key of Winston's dashboard. The engine sank to silence. So was the long haul over, and we had reached the end of 'The Autumn Road'.